The Imagination Box:
Beyond Infinity

Martyn Ford

FABER & FABER

For top parents, Barbara and Mick

First published in 2016
by Faber & Faber Limited
Bloomsbury House, 74–77 Great Russell Street
London, WC1B 3DA

Typeset in Garamond by M Rules
Printed and bound by CPI Group (UK) Ltd, Croydon, CR0 4YY

A CIP record for this book is available from the British Library

ISBN 978-0-571-31167-5

FSC
www.fsc.org
MIX
Paper from
responsible sources
FSC® C101712

2 4 6 8 10 9 7 5 3 1

Imagination is more important than knowledge. For knowledge is limited, whereas imagination embraces the entire world, stimulating progress, giving birth to evolution. It is, strictly speaking, a real factor in scientific research.

ALBERT EINSTEIN

Chapter 1

The Dawn Star Hotel's sign was bold, glowing through the grey air. Heavy hats of fresh snow, orange under spotlights, sat atop it. The bronze D, in particular, was creaking under the weight – a small gust was all it took to dislodge the letter, causing it to lean and fall.

Inside, in reception, Elisa flinched at the deep thud. After a swift inspection outside, she stomped back through the hotel's new revolving doors, shaking away the chill.

'The D's snapped off,' she said. 'The place is falling apart. I'm getting the builders to look at that too. It could have killed someone.'

'What's that?' Tim said, from the sofa in the lobby.

He didn't look up – his hand continued flowing left and right as he shaded a picture in his sketchpad.

'It's just outrageous. "The 'awn Star Hotel?" What next?'

'The A?' Tim suggested, changing his pencil for another.

Unimpressed, Elisa disappeared through the tall oak doors, deeper into the building. Tim put his feet up on the small coffee table in front of him – tilting his head, inspecting his work. The hotel's reception was huge, in fact you could probably fit an average-sized house in there and it wouldn't touch the sides. Tim enjoyed a big room – it was as though the further he could see the clearer he could think. This was no more so than at night when he would look up at the stars.

His thick sketchpad, perched on his lap, was open on an incredibly detailed picture of a tortoise. Not just any tortoise, no – this was Astro-Turtle, The Shelled Cosmonaut. And it was good work, Tim thought, adding a final reflection to the visor with the corner of his rubber. He'd drawn enough for today, so he shut the pad, put it under his arm and headed for his bedroom.

In the hall, Tim was greeted by a ripping noise that echoed all the way to the stairwell. Two decorators were tugging up the last strips of carpet, the dust making him think of a vacuum cleaner as he resisted the brewing tickle of a sneeze.

The patterned carpet – which Tim had spent much of his youth hopping up and down, pretending the red parts were lava and the spirals were stepping stones – was going. It was to be replaced, he had been told, by well-polished floorboards. The hotel was growing up.

Not letting the very literal demise of fond memories bother him too much, Tim went up to the second floor and into his bedroom – his sanctuary. It used to be just another guest suite but, besides the layout, it was now unrecognisable as a hotel room. Colourful and messy, it was decorated and cobbled together with artwork and things he had created in his imagination box: his clapper lamp, his glow-in-the-dark clock, the bubble machine, Merry Monkey

Circus (a doll's-house-sized tent of fun for Phil) and everything in between.

You see, during last year's summer holidays, a man called Professor George Eisenstone had stayed at the Dawn Star Hotel. As a consequence of being pretty curious Tim had found his invention: the imagination box. This is, basically, a gadget that creates whatever the user is imagining. Things like, say, a pencil or party poppers or a self-aware, talking finger monkey called Phil. Pop the reader (a hatty type thing that downloads your thoughts) on your noggin, picture what you want and, bam, there it is. Tim had even used the contraption to create his *own* imagination box. Clever. Like wishing for more wishes. To date, however, he was still the only person who could successfully operate the device.

Some other stuff happened too. There was a jetpack, some goo, a few robotic bees, the occasional explosion and even a monster at one point. Now though, things had simmered down and normality was the order of the day. Good, old-fashioned, monotonous normality.

Elisa – who ran the hotel – was reverting back to

some of her old ways too. There had been a distance between Tim and her in the past and the summer's events had certainly brought them closer. Even though he would now refer to her as his mother if someone asked – something he *never* used to do as he was, in fact, adopted – she would still sometimes appear detached and hopelessly preoccupied with managing the hotel. And her partner, Chris – he was just as absent as always.

Elisa's newest focus, and therefore source of sustained stress, was the refurbishment of the Dawn Star. However, her frenzied renovations hadn't infected Tim's bedroom – it was just as it had always been. This really was his cave. A place that would always be *his*, would always—

BANG: the door swung open. Elisa waddled in backwards, holding a large cardboard box with candlesticks and plates and other such clutter jutting out at wild angles.

'Tim,' she huffed, setting it down. 'We're going to put a couple of things in here while we wallpaper the top floors. I hope that's all right.'

This was *not* all right. 'What about all the other

space in this huge building?' Tim asked.

'We can't give up a guest room – you know we need the money.'

'I see.'

Tim was not happy with this idea, but he knew she was unlikely to change her mind. Once she had an idea in her head, Elisa was unstoppable. Although he understood she generally meant well, it still sometimes felt like the Dawn Star was her number one priority. Meaning Tim came in at a close second place.

'It'll only be for a few days, and only a couple of things.' She paused in the doorway, looking back. 'Is that all right?'

'You've kind of already started.' He pointed to the first box.

'Great, I'll let the boys know.'

Within half an hour, Tim's room was full. New corridors had been created by bulging boxes – carefully constructed pathways of floor. He had a narrow route to his bed, his desk, his door and to his window. Every other inch of space was occupied.

His sanctuary had become Elisa's dumping ground.

Sandwiched in his bed, Tim didn't sleep well – it was the last night of the Christmas holidays and the Sunday blues kept him clinging on to the last few hours of freedom. And when the faded rays of winter sun cut a square around his curtains, his unusual alarm was activated ...

'Goooood morning.' Phil sang loud, clicking along with his tiny fingers. 'Young Timothy, it's time for you to rise. Oh such a wonderful, glorious day.'

Tim grumbled into his pillow. 'What tune is that?'

'I have made it up,' the finger monkey continued to sing. 'Made it up to wake, wake, waaa-aake you up.'

'No,' Tim moaned. 'It has to stop.'

'Wooo-ah – we're halfway there ... Wooo-ah – wrestling grizzly bears.'

'This song doesn't even make sense. I am awake.'

Phil deflated. 'Are you not enjoying it?'

'It's just ... terrible. Deranged. Maybe even offensive.'

'Oh,' Phil said. 'It was merely my heartfelt way of saying good morning.' He bowed.

'Is it really though?' At times like this, Tim

wondered why he hadn't created Phil to be the kind of creature that liked lie-ins.

'Yes of course, Timothy, back to school today,' he said, pacing along the bedside cabinet. 'Where is your zest for life, sir? Why are you not more excited?'

'Reasons beside disliking early mornings and disliking school?'

'But school is a wonderful place, full of intrigue and knowledge, things to see, things to learn, things—'

'You have no idea what it is like. It's not all sunshine and sing-alongs,' Tim said. 'It's easy for you to be so optimistic – you can just think of a rainbow and you're in a good mood.'

'Now you are dramatically simplifying the nuanced, introspective correlation …' A broad smile spread across Phil's face.

'You're thinking about rainbows, aren't you?'

'They are just so colourful, and strange,' the monkey yelled, grinning with teeth. 'Ponder them. Go on. Heavens, how do they even work?'

'Refraction.'

'Tim!' Elisa shrieked through his door. 'Are you awake? Tim—'

'Yes, I'm awake,' he shouted. 'I'm awake.' Whispering now. 'I'm so very awake.'

He got up and dressed in his new school blazer, then slung his rucksack over his shoulder. It was still early enough for the hands on his clock to glow.

'Right,' Tim said. 'I've got to go.'

Phil was sitting on the desk, distracted by his own knees. 'So, so useful.'

Rolling his eyes and smiling, Tim left the room. He made his way downstairs and paused in the hallway with a sigh.

The carpet was now completely gone.

Nodding to himself, he continued. He had to be careful, because these weren't just normal floorboards – no, this was the deck of a vast ship, a frigate, and a storm was abrewin'. He steadied himself on the handrail as waves thrashed and roared up at his sides, great cliffs of black water blocked the horizon, and salty spray rained down on him as fellow pirates rallied around the ropes and secured the sail. They

9

needed to … Oh, what's the point, Tim thought, looking down at his feet.

This was just a regular wooden floor.

It was quiet in the lobby. However, outside, a man wearing a black leather jacket was standing perfectly still in the light snow, staring through the window into the hotel. Perhaps a potential guest, Tim reasoned.

'The bus is going to be here in three minutes, Tim,' Elisa said, tugging on his tie. 'What is … what kind of knot *is* this?' She undid it, then started looping it back around.

Tim wasn't paying much attention – instead, he was looking over her shoulder at that man who was making eye contact now. He had the strangest expression on his face, as though he was sleepwalking or something.

'You know that guy?' Tim said, shuffling out of his view.

'What's that?'

'That … man. Behind you.'

When she turned, however, he was gone. 'There's

no one there.'

'I ...' That's weird, Tim thought, double-checking through the glass.

'Got your maths book?' Elisa said, bringing his gaze back.

'Yes.'

'Lunch money?' Now she was interfering with his collar.

'Yes.'

'Pencil case?'

'Yes.'

'Did you do your science homework?'

Tim's eyes widened. 'Um ... yes?'

'Oh, Tim,' Elisa sighed. 'One piece of homework over Christmas, *one piece.*'

She was right. One piece, so easy and so straightforward Tim didn't even need to worry about it. Or think about it. Or remember it. Or do it.

'How long until the bus gets here?' he asked, placing his bag on the floor.

'Two minutes now.'

'Plenty of time.'

11

Tim turned and barrelled down the corridor – the wood was charmless, and loud, under his feet. Three stairs at a time, yanking at the banister, up to his room. Straight to his cupboard, straight to his imagination box. He put the reader on, the hat that will extract his thoughts and send his creation to the contraption, then closed his eyes as the box gently rumbled and fizzled away.

'Bye, Phil,' Tim said, whipping the freshly cooked homework from the sleek metal device. Back in the lobby, he swung his bag on his shoulder and made for the exit.

Elisa spotted the sheet of paper, realising what he'd done. 'I'm *pretty* sure that's cheating.'

'Is it?' Tim said, stepping backwards.

'Well, it'll be interesting to see what mark you get,' she said.

Tim laughed, pressing himself into the swivel door. 'I imagine I'll get an A.'

Chapter 2

The following morning Tim stepped off the bus and headed through the front gates of Glassbridge Academy – high, navy blue iron railings and cobblestones conjured images of an old-fashioned prison. He passed a cluster of disproportionately tall, dim-faced Year 11s huddled in a circle.

Today his bag was particularly heavy as it contained something that it most certainly should not have contained – his imagination box. Swallowing, he glared at fellow pupils and staff as he went, trying his best not to appear suspicious. The decision to bring the contraption into school was not taken lightly. In fact, the day before, he had given it a great deal of thought ...

Tim's vision had been falling in and out of focus. Sitting at the back of the classroom, by the window, he had been leaning in his chair, enjoying long, teary-eyed yawns.

'Well done, Jeremy,' Mrs Willis had said, placing a sheet of paper on a desk at the front of the room. 'Simon, Vanessa, Thomas,' she'd continued, dropping work on each table as she went. 'Good efforts all round.'

His tall teacher had stopped in front of Tim, tilting her folder and looking over her thick black glasses. Tim waited, growing ever so slightly nervous. This had been a last-ditch attempt, this homework he'd quickly imagined into existence. It was only then, when Mrs Willis was about to deliver the marked paper to him, that he started to wonder whether or not it could be passed off as *his* work. He silently wished he'd actually read it before handing it in . . .

'. . . and Tim,' she said, sounding confused, 'you got . . . one hundred per cent. Well done.'

He nodded, pleased to have got away with it, despite his suspicious mark. Generally, when he remembered to do his homework, Tim's score would be slightly above average, but rarely *this* good. He was described by more than one teacher as 'full of potential'. This, Tim concluded, was a positive way of saying he could, and therefore should, do better at school.

But, the real fact was, school wasn't that much fun. Even art, Tim's favourite subject, had its downsides. When tasked with drawing something, he felt a sudden urge to draw literally *anything* else. Especially when it was a choice between sketching some apples and bananas on the desk or, say, a demon-biker hedgehog wizard named Sir Nicholas of Fiddleberry.

The words 'This is very good, Tim. *However …*' appeared at the bottom of almost every picture in his school sketchpad.

Tim turned to the window and flinched – grabbing his heart – when he saw Mr Muldoon standing there, looking right at him. Hesitating, Tim waved, then returned his attention to the desk. Out of the corner of his eye, he noticed the headteacher wander off across the playground. He briefly wondered if he had something on his face – this was the second time someone had stared at him like that. It was getting creepy.

Slightly unsettled, Tim then slipped back into his thoughts. Now ... now this revelation, this way of getting good – no, great, no, *perfect* – grades with virtually no effort would change things forever. He hadn't even considered using the imagination box to do his homework before, but now it seemed so obvious. Another cunning idea had sparked in his head – what if he did *all* his schoolwork in the imagination box? Of course, that'd mean bringing it in his bag, which had been expressly forbidden. Although Elisa and Chris knew about the device, and about Phil, there were still very strict rules about it being kept secret from the rest of the world. Professor Eisenstone had told him never to take it from his *bedroom*, let alone out of the building.

He shook the thought away and decided, there in the classroom, that he mustn't. There was no way he could, it was too wrong. It was breaking too many rules. However, during that first gruelling Monday of term – when the clock's ticks seemed to be slowing down as the day went on – Tim steadily changed his mind. As long as he was extra careful, he told himself, then it'd be just fine and dandy.

And so, Tuesday, here he was with his imagination box safely stowed away in his rucksack and a dim ache in his shoulder from the new weight. He strode fast along the side of the school, then turned towards the long tarmac path that led to the playground.

Dee was sitting, hunched over, looking down at her phone, on the small brick wall that rounded the edge of the building. As Tim approached, she lifted her head for a smile, but then her attention went straight back to her mobile.

Since last summer, Tim and Dee had become best friends – even more so now they'd started secondary school together. However, while they were certainly close, she was sometimes a little cold. She didn't mean to be and Tim had long since learned it was nothing personal – she just had a very logical outlook and was sometimes quite direct with her words.

This also meant that she was impervious to negative comment. When a rat-themed wrong'n called Johnny

Harrington in Year 9 called her 'Dot to Dot' as she often wore polka-dot clothing, and everyone laughed, Dee simply ignored it. She said that she considered feeling sad, but decided not to. Sometimes Tim wished he could be more like her, wished he could see the world in such objective terms and choose how he felt about it.

He sat by her side on the wall and, as he glanced through the chain-link fence to the playground, Mr Muldoon strolled past and met his gaze. 'Dee, listen,' Tim said, leaning towards her, becoming genuinely unnerved by these people staring at him, 'something unusual is going on, I—'

'Check this out,' she said. On the screen was an animated squirrel, riding a snowboard. It was the intro to a popular game, set to a catchy song, which Dee was humming along to.

'Squirrel Boarder,' Tim said. 'I've seen this.'

'Yeah, sure, but have you seen it on the IcoRama 2020?' Dee said, proudly flipping her phone over. Only then did Tim realise it was brand new.

'That's very nice.'

Christmas had been particularly disappointing for Tim this year. What do you get for the boy who can have anything in an instant?

Elisa chose socks.

'Do I see the green eyes of envy?' Dee asked. 'It's an IcoRama ... the newest one. Everyone on earth has one, or wants one. It'd be understandable if you wanted one too.'

'Dee, trust me, if I wanted one, I'd have one.'

And this was the crux; this was what Tim had spent the last few months battling against. Whilst, on paper, having *anything* you want seems great, in practice it gets dull far quicker than you might expect. The paradox of possession, Eisenstone had called it.

It's *just stuff*, Tim always found himself thinking.

Sighing, he then thought of the red carpet at the hotel disappearing.

'Are you all right?' Dee asked. 'Looking kinda glum there.'

'There's just ... there's just no lava any more.'

'Doesn't *really* make sense, in the context of this

conversation …' Dee said. 'I know, make something new and you'll feel better.'

'Hmm. I don't know.'

'Remember on the news, remember all that looting?' Dee said. 'People were breaking into shops to steal trainers, laptops, all sorts. Why? Because new things rock.'

There had been riots in a number of towns across the country a few weeks prior – there were even some disturbances in Glassbridge, usually a quaint, sleepy place.

'What's your point?'

'That creating something new will cheer you up. Look, why do you think people work? For money – so they can buy nice things. Everyone's at it. You just get to skip the work bit, hurrah.'

'It's just—'

'*It's just stuff*,' Dee interrupted, in a mocking voice. He'd said this to her more than once over the summer, during which he'd spent hours making things for her – clothes, toys, gadgets. You name it, she'd got it: bespoke desires sated instantly with virtually no effort. Tim had watched the technology change her – it had made her notably materialistic, far more so than when they first met. This was another reason his love for the machine had lessened. Perhaps if she had one, she would understand.

'You know, Tim, most kids our age would *kill* for their own imagination box. When was the last time you made yourself something you *really* wanted?' She wiggled her IcoRama.

It was a long time ago, Tim realised. And he'd deliberately avoided making himself a phone. It was as though a modern mobile, the ultimate possession according to everyone at school, would be the final creation. Then he really *would* have everything.

'Would you be satisfied if I made myself a phone?' Tim said. 'Fine.'

He reached into his bag, pulled out his reader – his black woollen beanie, the letters 'TIB' printed small on the front – and put it on his head.

'Nice hat,' Johnny Harrington said, weaving past on a small silver scooter.

'Thank you.' Tim ignored the sarcasm.

'Tim?' Dee leant away, then checked over her shoulder. 'You've brought it into *school*?' she whispered.

'Yes, I can rustle up my work with it.'

'That's cheating, that is ... Oh. I knew it. One hundred per cent on your science, you wily scamp.'

'Scamp?'

'Hey, hang on. Can you do my work?'

'Now that definitely *is* cheating,' Tim said.

He closed his eyes for a second, then reached back into his school bag and removed a brand-new, shiny, top-of-the-range IcoRama 2020 mobile. Hundreds of pounds worth of groundbreaking, touch-screen brilliance. The back was engraved, 'Tim's phone'.

'Is your life better now?' Dee asked. 'It is, isn't it? Granddad needs to be getting his act together. It's about time I had me one of these imagination boxes.'

Tim slid it into his pocket, then took the reader off. He shimmied closer to her. 'Anyway, something weird is going on,' he said. 'People ... people keep ... staring at me.'

'What kind of people?'

'People, Mr Muldoon, a random guy in the street. It's happened a few times.'

'You're a handsome young man, you should be flattered.'

'Somehow, I don't think that's the reason,' Tim said.

Wednesday morning and Phil was lying with his hand behind his head and his feet crossed in the middle of Tim's pillow, flicking through the TV channels. The remote, perched on his knees, was more than twice his size.

The television blurted out nonsensical sounds as he clicked from one station to the next.

'Hang on,' Tim said. 'Go back. That was Glassbridge.'

'The news?' Phil went back two channels.

'Yeah, what were they talking about?'

A reporter was standing in a supermarket, near the vegetables. 'It is truly a bemusing situation,' the woman said, holding her microphone at her chest. 'Here, in a large superstore in Glassbridge, it is clear that something is missing – and what is it? Carrots. That's right, up and down the country people have been panic-buying carrots – a bizarre fad which has seen stores boost prices and carrots become, almost overnight, the most sought-after vegetable.'

'Hmm,' Tim said.

'It was initially thought to be an internet prank that went viral. However that is yet to be confirmed,' the reporter added. 'All we can be sure of is that shoppers of Great Britain will do almost anything to get their hands on this humble vegetable.' She lifted a carrot in view of the camera, and took a bite. 'I'm Samantha Locke, for GBW News, live from Glassbridge. Back to you in the studio.'

'Well, my word,' Phil said, stroking his furry chin. 'How very strange.'

Chapter 3

For the next few weeks, Tim took his imagination box to school every single day. He would do odd bits of work himself but, for the vast majority of the time, he would take the easy road. He even varied the quality, so no one would suspect a thing.

The final bell rang through Glassbridge Academy on a chilly Friday – the last day before half-term – and Tim strode towards the gates with a familiar empty feeling. Outside, the new snow had all but melted – the piles of thickly packed ice at the edge of roads and paths had become dirty and brown. The best of winter was gone.

Tim headed out of the school grounds to see the bus driver standing in front of his double-decker, scratching his head and talking on his mobile phone. Steam was spurting, hissing out of the grill – clearly, the bus had broken down.

Luckily, the Dawn Star wasn't too far to walk, so Tim wandered off towards the main road. It was market day, and the town centre was packed. The high street had been transformed into a loud, vibrant place – florists shouted deals about tulips, and one stallholder yelled something in what sounded like another language before adding, 'Pound o' bananas!' The hot smell of smoky, fried food – burgers, sausages, sweet onions – sizzled and fogged from a nearby van. To his right a band was setting up – one member was polishing his trumpet and another was unravelling a wire.

'He's real,' a crazed voice announced to his left. 'The Mind Surfer is real!' Tim saw a scruffy preacher handing out leaflets in the entrance to a chemist. He looked homeless. 'Purge yourself of this evil,' he sang. 'Free yourself from the grip of control, free your *miiiind*.'

Lot of weirdos in Glassbridge, Tim thought, as he meandered along.

On that subject, he remembered the previous year – the investigation, finding and rescuing Eisenstone, the nightmare that still gave him shivers, Clarice's twisted psyche finding its way into the real world and destroying Crowfield House. That monster she accidently created in her huge imagination box – the demon that passed through Tim's mind. An image he didn't think he would ever forget.

Tim's pace slowed, almost to a standstill.

Through the uprights of the stripy market canopies, the plastic sheets bulging in the wind like sails and winter-dressed figures criss-crossing past each another, Tim saw another person staring at him. Just like the leather-jacketed man at the hotel, just like Mr Muldoon. Even when someone blocked his line of sight, the man remained in place, peering through the available gaps. He didn't move. He didn't blink.

He just watched.

Unnerved by the stranger, Tim changed course and turned to his right, to head down an alleyway. He was worried enough by this unusual, and yet increasingly familiar, sight to think it a good idea to steer well clear. As he rounded the corner, past some bins, he had a quick glance over his shoulder, back towards the high street. At any rate, whatever was going on, the man hadn't followed him, which was something to be grateful—

Tim stopped dead.

Another man was right in front of him now, blocking the path. He was dressed in a grey blazer, with a red silk tie, a bowler hat and was leaning on his closed umbrella, as though it was a walking stick.

Neither of them said anything. Tim listened to the sounds of the market behind, muffled now by the distance, near silent in fact. And then the man, who had no emotion on his face – nothing in his cold, empty eyes – held out his hand and spoke four crystal-clear words.

'Give me the box.'

In the narrow alleyway, Tim very carefully curled his arm behind him, lifting the remaining strap on to his shoulder so that he was wearing his school rucksack properly, the imagination box tucked safely inside. The suited man didn't move. He just waited with his hand open between them. After a few seconds, Tim found the courage to respond.

'Excuse me?' Tim said. A pause. 'What box?'

'Give me the box,' the man said again.

Letting out a slow, jittery breath, Tim pulled on his bag's straps, tightening them. Handing over the imagination box just simply wasn't an option.

'I think,' Tim said, frowning, 'I'm going to go with ... no?'

He took a step away and, as if a switch had been hit, the man lurched forwards, the bowler hat flipping off his head. With this, Tim spun round and ran.

Coming back on to the high street, Tim's feet hit the pavement hard and fast. He turned down the road, bolting through the packed market. Scared, confused, he felt that running away was a very reasonable short-term solution to this situation.

'Hey, watch it,' a passerby huffed as he weaved through the shoppers.

A quick glance behind, Tim saw the man was gaining on him. With a hard skid and a breathy 'sorry', Tim shouldered into the corner of a stall, changing course. The whole thing swayed, mobile-phone cases and accessories swung, some falling from their display.

'Hey!' the owner yelled, but Tim was already making good speed along the path behind the stalls. Again, though, the pursuer was gaining.

Another sharp corner and Tim was leaping through the band. He knocked into the singer, who yelped down the microphone. The trumpet player – wide-eyed – blew out a weird, surprised note.

'Whoops, excuse me,' Tim said, still at full speed.

The chaos drifted out of focus as he continued, leaving the market behind. He swung his legs over a pedestrian railing, into the road, spinning, holding his palms out to traffic that screeched to a stop all around him – one car thumped hard into the back of another. Motorists were yelling, gesturing wildly with their hands.

'Oh God, I am properly sorry,' Tim said, still running.

This commotion put some good distance between them and, a little further down the next street, Tim saw an opportunity to lose his pursuer entirely. The city's wide river was directly up ahead, with a large tourist boat approaching the drawbridge. The lights were all on and the familiar bell was dinging. A section of road split in the middle, two halves lifting away from each other. His plan was simple – he would jump the gap.

Swooping under the barrier, Tim ignored the shouts of a concerned passerby. He made his way along the pavement, which was lifting more and more, turning into an ever steeper hill. The water below was dark grey and the packed boat full of passengers, some beginning to take notice, fingers pointing, was passing under the raised bridge.

Tim scrambled the last few metres to the top and jumped. Kicking through the empty air between the two ramps, he only just passed the gap, landing awkwardly on his side on the opposite slope. He slid, rolling, scraping, towards the barriers below.

Looking back, he knew there was no way the man could follow him now, the space was far too wide. He caught his breath, ignoring the shocked onlookers, some of whom were filming him on their phones. Tim had to blink and do a double take when he spotted the man across the water. Still with his eyes fixed on Tim, he was clambering over the railing. He stood for a short moment at the river's edge.

Tim gasped, covering his mouth in horror, as the man stepped off the wall, falling into the dark, freezing water below. Light blue bubbles flowered on the surface where he'd gone in, and then he burst up, taking a desperate gulp of air.

'Ah!' the man screamed, seeming confused. 'Where am I? Cold!'

He turned and swam back to the safety ladder and clambered out, shivering. He didn't seem to care about Tim any more – it was as though the shock of the water had snapped him out of a trance. People rushed to the man's aid, and one helper removed his jacket to wrap around his shuddering shoulders. After a few seconds, Tim stepped away from the river – his mind was racing, his eyes darting as he tried to work out what on earth was going on.

He travelled round the corner on to a path that

led to Glassbridge Park, checking behind again. But, when he looked back, a woman was blocking his path.

'Give me the box,' she said. She was wearing a high-visibility jacket and Tim quickly realised she was a lollipop lady.

'What? Again?' he said, his chest still aching from the chase. 'Are you joking?'

'Give me the box,' she said, in a monotone. Tim noticed that, like the last man, she had a completely vacant, dead-eyed expression.

Now more exhausted than confused, he sighed and shrugged. 'No,' he said.

The woman grabbed him by the scruff of the neck, but he shook her off and, again, was running. Having warmed up, he found he was able to sprint at an extreme speed. He burst through the bushes at the edge of the park, crossed a street and swept into Glassbridge Mall – a vast, brightly lit shopping centre.

His breathing, pounding heart and sore muscles were throbbing in unison as he ran, thinking that, no matter what happened, he needed to keep hold of the box. Up ahead was the exit. This was the home straight – once he was outside the mall, he would easily be able to dart down one of the many alleyways and lose his second pursuer of the day. He just had to pass through the wide-open glass doors: he leant forwards, gritting his teeth and pushing his legs harder and faster than he'd—

Thwack.

Well, it would appear that the doors were, in fact, closed.

He was now stumbling backwards as the huge pane of reinforced glass, which had been cleaned *too well* in his opinion, wobbled from the impact. His eyes dipped and fell shut as the ground seemed to tilt up towards him. He was aware of the cold floor on his cheek as the lollipop lady's boots stepped over – her hands reached inside his rucksack and removed the imagination box. Helpless and dizzy, he drifted away from consciousness, peacefully appreciating how nice it feels to fall asleep.

Chapter 4

'They say you might get a little confused,' Elisa said, touching his hair. Tim was in bed, back at home, with no recollection of how he'd got there.

Distant memories, like forgotten dreams, were at the edge of his mind. There had been people standing over him in a circle, looking down, concerned. Beyond them Tim had seen the shopping centre's ceiling – it had looked a mile away.

'You bumped your head,' Elisa added. 'It's not serious, but you do need to rest. The doctor said you have mild concussion.'

'What happened?' Tim vaguely remembered some strange music and for some reason he was angry with a window cleaner. 'Do you know any window cleaners?'

'We've discussed this, a few times. You ran into some very clean glass. Just rest, Tim, you'll feel better soon.' Elisa's phone buzzed in her pocket. She stood and answered it. 'Hello, yes … How much? For little single packets of jam?' Pacing, she sighed at whoever was on the other end. 'It's too expensive. It's madness.'

She left to settle a dispute about the price of jam. This was typical Elisa – summoned away, back to work, like a yo-yo.

Tim watched the TV and frowned at the uncomfortable ache in the centre of his head. The news came on. They were still talking about the riots that happened weeks ago. Volunteers had helped repaint the front of a shop that was damaged. He recognised the reporter – she had short rusty-red hair and a slim face with defined cheekbones. At the end of her report, she said, 'I'm Samantha Locke, for GBW News.'

Phil was sitting on the bedside cabinet, slouching into the black material of Tim's reader hat. He'd been rambling for a while now.

'... rambunctious kind of creatures, aren't they? What about big cats?' he asked. 'I mean, is a cheetah a leopard?'

'No,' Tim said.

'What is a cheetah then?'

'A cheetah is a cheetah.'

'So ... what is a leopard?'

'A leopard.'

'Hmm. Let us just agree to disagree.'

'No, they're different ... I ...' Tim scrunched his eyes as fragments began to reform ... Something about a box. The market. The man. The bridge. Someone else. A bright lady. *Lollipop*. It all came flooding back. 'My hat,' he said, noticing it was underneath the monkey.

Tim swung his legs out of bed, glancing around the floor. He spotted his school bag on his swivel chair and unzipped it. Two workbooks and a flattened chocolate-bar wrapper, nothing else. Illogically, he turned it upside down and shook it, half hoping his vision was playing tricks on him.

'It's gone,' he said, staring at the wall, unable to

process the information. 'The imagination box. That woman stole it. Or someone. People were chasing me, Phil. First a man, in a suit. Oh, it's hazy, but he ... he jumped in the river. I jumped over the bridge.' Tim rubbed his forehead.

'It is quite customary for sufferers of concussion to talk nonsense,' Phil concluded.

'Oh this is so, so bad.'

'How bad?'

'The baddest.'

'Hang on a moment. Young Timothy, are you telling me the imagination box, which you have been mischievously taking to school, has been stolen?'

'Yes.'

'Oh my. A pickle, you might say. But never mind, you said you were getting bored of it anyway.'

'This is serious.' Tim felt horribly responsible – this was a direct consequence of breaking the rules. 'What if it falls into the wrong hands? You remember last summer. Right. OK. We've got to find it.'

'Perhaps you should tell the professor.'

Oh no, Tim thought, *Eisenstone*. As much as he

hated to admit it, Phil was right. 'He's ... he's not going to like this news.'

He leapt into his jeans, threw on his red-chequered shirt and body warmer before doing his laces and, finally, placing his reader hat on. Now it purely served to keep his head from catching a chill – nothing more. Outside, light powdery snow – the third batch this winter – was falling fast but, sadly, not settling.

'Right, are you ready?' Tim asked. 'Phil?'

'So what, pray tell, is a puma?' the monkey said, looking up and noticing Tim was fully dressed. 'Oh ding dong jolly jack – are we going somewhere nice?'

'We're going to Eisenstone's.'

'Oh yes, of course.'

Tim clicked his fingers and Phil scurried up the bedside lamp's neck and leapt on to his arm, before nestling in the top pocket of Tim's shirt.

'What about the concussion?' Phil asked.

'The what?'

'You must be completely better.'

*

'Ah, hello, Tim,' Professor Eisenstone said, opening the door. 'Come on in, you must be freezing. Indeed, snow ... *snow* day to be outside.'

Tim had cycled here, his back wheel leaving a curved skid in the gravel of Eisenstone's driveway. Thick lungfuls of steam puffed from his mouth as he caught his breath.

The professor had light stubble and bags under his eyes. He'd been working hard recently. In the months since the Crowfield House incident, Eisenstone had returned to his efforts on the imagination box. He was in the process of creating the next prototype – one he said that would be equipped with safety restrictions, ensuring the user couldn't accidently, or deliberately, create a nightmare monster, or torrents of fire, or some ghastly airborne disease that makes people turn inside out. Also, the next version would, he insisted, be fit for 'everyone' to use. This, Tim knew, was a day Dee was very much looking forward to.

The professor had, more than once, hinted at the dangers of the imagination box being too severe for Tim. He'd never actually said so, but Tim could tell

Eisenstone didn't really like the idea of him owning the device. So he was both curious and terrified to see how he would react to the news that it was now gone.

Ducking under his arm, Tim stepped inside. He went straight into the professor's lounge, which now reminded him of his own bedroom. The clutter was immense – the sheer volume of electronics, circuitry and various components was staggering. In the corner was a huge metal box, like a stand-alone cash machine, covered in wires, exposed transistors and light bulbs.

'So, how's school?' Eisenstone said, following him in and heading straight to the prototype.

'Um … yeah … rubbish. Borderline torture.' Tim was thinking how best to explain the situation. What he'd done with his box – taking it out of his room – had been explicitly, repeatedly forbidden. For, it seemed, good reason.

'Oh, now, now, now, I am sure it's not that bad.' The professor was fiddling with the contraption – it was clear that Tim had arrived in the middle of testing.

'It's not all skipping ropes and marbles nowadays, Eisenstone, school's different.'

'Indeed, I assure, sure, sure you, school was no picnic in my day,' he said. 'They used to, well, they used to hit you with a stick if you misbehaved.' He glanced over his shoulder with a handful of cables hanging from his fingers like spaghetti. 'And they used to make you play football in your pants if you forgot your PE kit. Even if you were wearing pants that had been, say, say, turned pink by a rogue red sock in the wash. Even then. Or some such equally devastating example.' He stared into space. 'Dark days indeed.'

'Yeah, fair enough, they don't do that sort of thing any more. What with the law and that.'

'Still, half-term now, isn't it. So, so, what can I do for you?'

Tim sat and shuffled on the sofa, his palms sweaty.

'Indeed, it must be said, I am actually in the thick of some rather compelling breakthroughs.' The professor stroked the machine, then fiddled with a bolt on the side. 'But it's very delicate work.'

Phil poked his head from the pocket.

'Oh yes, hello, Phil,' Eisenstone said, flicking a switch and turning to face them. 'I didn't see you there.'

'Good day, sir.' The monkey leapt on to the arm of the sofa.

Tim's leg was vibrating as he chewed on his thumbnail.

'So,' the professor continued, 'do you know what's plaguing Tim's mind?'

'I feel I do,' Phil said, pouting and nodding with half-shut eyes. 'Young Timothy would like to discuss the differences and similarities between African and Asian large-cat species.'

'No,' Tim said. 'That's not why I'm here.'

'Have you just come, come, come to see the new prototype?' The professor proudly jutted a thumb over his shoulder at the complicated device behind him. Right then Tim noticed that one of the circuit boards was glowing. Then, with a flicker, a small flame quickly licked up the side. Within a second it doubled in size. 'I think I've cracked it, it's all coming together quite beautifully. *Beautifully.*'

'It is on fire,' Phil said, pointing.

Gasping, the professor spun round and blasted the machine with a long spray from a small red fire extinguisher – the corner of the room disappeared in a cloud of CO_2. He opened a window and gathered up some tools.

'Right,' Tim said, lifting his gaze. He hoped to slip the confession in amid the chaos. 'I …' He clenched his teeth, feeling the cold air and smelling the smoke – it reminded him of a hairdryer. All at once he felt biting guilt about what he'd done. What on earth had he been playing at? The sudden self-doubt took him by surprise. 'Look, I did something I shouldn't have …'

'*Oh*,' Phil said, rolling his eyes. 'That. Yes, Professor, Timothy has been taking the imagination box to school and now he has lost it.'

Tim glared at the monkey, both angry and kind of relieved that he'd blurted it out.

Eisenstone took a moment to react. First he nodded, then his eyes opened further as he glanced between Tim and Phil. 'Indeed? Is, is, is this true?'

'Yes,' Tim said. 'I … I took the imagination box to school, and, I—'

'But why?' Eisenstone's cheeks flashed pink. He didn't look angry as such, but rather as though he just couldn't believe it. His attention was now all on Tim – he seemed to have forgotten about the recent fire. 'What . . . what *possible* reason . . .?'

'I started doing my homework in it. With it. Then all my work.'

The scientist in Eisenstone got the better of him as a slight smile crossed his face. 'How, how have your grades been?'

'Much better,' Tim said, the mood momentarily lightened. 'I wondered if it was cheating, but the answers are coming from *my* brain, so I suppose not.'

'Indeed, but are they?' The professor looked animated. 'Do you *know* the atomic make-up of all the things you've created – the jetpack, your own imagination box, a finger monkey? It is plausible you're tapping into something we don't yet understand. A universal, collective consciousness, perhaps bleeding into your subconscious . . . it's *infinitely* exciting— Wait, and you *lost* the box?!'

'Worse,' Tim said. 'It was stolen. By a lollipop lady.'

'*A lollipop lady?*' The professor tapped his index finger on his chin.

After a grand breath, Tim explained the whole afternoon. The mysterious man who leapt into the river, the lollipop lady, getting knocked out, everything. 'But I *promise* I'll find it,' Tim said. 'I double promise.'

'You ... you promised you wouldn't take it out of your room,' Eisenstone said with a sad disappointment that made Tim want to cry.

'I know. I am sorry.'

'Tim,' the professor said, standing amid the low white fog from the fire extinguisher, a few dim lights glowing behind him. 'I think I know who can help us.'

Chapter 5

In the car, as Tim watched the motorway zip past the window, he remembered the conversation he'd had with Dee, before he created his mobile phone. Now that his imagination box had been stolen, he *longed* for it. Only a few weeks before he'd been wondering if it was a curse, not a gift, to have anything he wanted. But now, he was—

'Oh,' Tim said to himself, as frustration shifted to simple sadness.

'What?' Eisenstone turned his head, keeping his eyes on the road in front of him. 'What is it?'

'Nothing, I just … I just remembered all the homework I've been set.' He'd have to do it the old-fashioned way.

They arrived at their destination a little over an hour later. The professor did his best to explain where they'd come. It was called the Diamond Building: the London headquarters of the Technology, Research and Defence (TRAD) agency, a discreet government organisation tasked with investigating and safeguarding new, potentially dangerous technology. It was set up, he said, following the invention of the atomic bomb.

Climbing out of Eisenstone's car, Tim turned and arched his neck to take in the vast, towering building. Clad in clean glass, it was the colour of the sky above, reflected clouds flowing from top to bottom, like water running down a slide. They walked past a huge, circular fountain and then through some tall, revolving doors. In the lobby, which was made from rich, glossy marble, Tim saw pairs of security guards posted at every available doorway. This place looked just as secret as Eisenstone said it was.

They were taken through a checkpoint and escorted down a long, plain hallway by a young man with a hands-free earpiece clipped to the side of his head. Then they arrived at a door – Eisenstone entered first. A woman stood up from her desk and stepped towards them. 'George, long time no see,' she said, before kissing his cheek. 'And this must be Timothy Hart.'

Tim smiled.

'Harriet Goffe,' the woman said, extending her hand for Tim to shake.

Harriet, the professor had explained in the car, was in charge. She was TRAD's director and the first port of call for the unexplained theft of Tim's imagination box. Eisenstone and she were old friends – she had been a student of his many years ago. However, they had become reacquainted last summer after the professor was kidnapped by Clarice Crowfield, who had been hell-bent on making her own imagination box work. As a consequence, TRAD now knew all about Tim and the technology. Understandably, the agency was particularly interested in its possible risks.

'And ...' Harriet stepped towards her internal window and twisted the stick on the slatted blinds, shutting them in. 'Would it be all right if I met Phil?'

Instinctively, Tim glanced to Eisenstone, who gave him a quick nod. The professor had explained that Harriet could be trusted, that TRAD might already have leads on a suspect.

'Phil,' Tim said.

The monkey scurried from his shirt pocket and up on to his shoulder. As people tend to, Harriet looked utterly astonished.

'My goodness,' she said, leaning in close.

She was middle-aged, with narrow eyes, thin lips and blonde hair neatly plaited and tied at the back – it was long enough to hang over her shoulder. Wearing a smart skirt with a brown blazer, she seemed somehow from the wrong decade, dressed in dated clothes. On her desk, Tim noticed an antique telephone – large and black, with one of those ridiculous circular number dialling things. What on earth were they thinking when they invented that, Tim wondered.

'Pleased to meet you,' Phil said and, right on cue, Harriet looked as though everything she'd ever known about the entire universe had just been turned on its head.

'I told you you'd be impressed,' Eisenstone said, smiling.

After the astonishment, disbelief and quizzing of Phil, the topic turned serious.

'So, Tim, what happened to the box?' she asked.

Tim recounted the story.

'It is perplexing,' Harriet said, after he had finished. 'We'll need to make some enquiries. Of course, as Eisenstone has no doubt told you, this technology – especially following the events of Crowfield House – is quite sought after.'

'Indeed.'

'There is a need to keep a close watch on you, Tim,' she said. 'After all, it's not long until whoever *did* steal your imagination box realises that it is useless without *you* as well. I wouldn't want to instil undue fear, Tim, but it is possible that the person responsible for this is ... dangerous. Have either of you ever heard of ... the Mind Surfer?'

Eisenstone shook his head.

'Um, yeah ... This guy, he was shouting something about that at the market,' Tim said. 'He seemed mad.'

He had assumed the preacher he'd seen was just peddling gibberish – in fact, he'd actually forgotten the incident altogether until Harriet mentioned the name.

'Hmm, yes. The Mind Surfer is a colloquial term for someone long thought to be a myth, a conspiracy theory popular on obscure internet forums,' she whispered, leaning forwards. 'You know, the kind of people who wear tinfoil hats and think Facebook can put adverts in your dreams. There have been rumours circulating that we are investigating – and this information must *not* leave this room.' She glared. 'Some people believe that the individual, or organisation, has created a device that allows them to *take control* of another person. To hijack them.'

'Wow,' Tim said. It reminded him of when Clarice Crowfield and Professor Whitelock had transmitted their thoughts through his mind.

'The man who chased you ... it seemed as though he "snapped out of it" when he went into the water?'

'Yes.'

'Did you recognise him? What was he wearing?'

'I …' Tim winced. 'I hit my head. I can only remember bits …'

There was a knock at the door.

'Mmm, yes,' Harriet said.

A man, in his thirties at Tim's guess, stepped inside. He had short brown hair and stubble on his face. He didn't seem at all surprised to see Eisenstone and Tim, but still said, 'Oh, am I interrupting? I left my jacket …'

'Not at all,' Harriet said. 'Fredric, this is Professor George Eisenstone. George, this is Fredric Wilde.'

'Oh, wow,' Fredric said, in an American accent. 'No introductions necessary. I have been following Professor Eisenstone's innovations for a long time. I was in Glassbridge last summer for your seminar … "There is a box …",' he said, beaming. 'I must say, dude, your work has been an *inspiration* to me and my company.'

The professor and Fredric shook hands. 'Oh yes, indeed. I am pleased.'

'I have a first edition of *Quantum World* – I'd be stoked if you could sign it for me.'

'Of course.'

Tim could see this man was extremely excited to meet Eisenstone.

'Do ... do you work for TRAD?' the professor asked.

'Uh, no, I—'

'Fredric has taken over one of our American facilities,' Harriet explained, sounding particularly well spoken now in comparison. 'We've had our funding cut – we've had to sell off a few of our larger buildings.'

'Oh, you gotta see what we're working on over there.' Fredric's eyes were blue enough to seem almost white. 'Anyway,' he said, grabbing his coat from a nearby hook. 'I'll leave you guys—'

He stopped, glancing for the first time at Tim or, rather, at his hand where Phil was sitting. 'What, exactly, is *that*?'

'Finger monkey,' Tim said.

'A talking one,' Phil added, turning his head.

Fredric closed the door behind him and stepped towards a chair. 'This is a conversation I'd very much like to be a part of,' he said.

A little later, Harriet escorted Eisenstone and Tim down one of the Diamond Building's long, narrow corridors. They were heading for the security department, to view CCTV footage of the imagination box's theft. They passed offices and laboratories, some of which were impossible to ignore.

'Timothy, are you familiar with the common misconception that the moon is made of cheese?' Phil asked. He was pleased to be somewhere he didn't have to remain hidden. 'Because I would like to disclose some musings on the matter.'

'Yes?'

'I am aware it is fictitious, but I assume there is *some* cheese on the surface – the myth cannot surely be absolute fabrication?'

'There is no cheese on the moon, not even a little bit . . . Look at this.' Tim stopped.

In the next room, through the viewing window, he

saw the remains of Clarice Crowfield's imagination box, the metal torn, buckled. And, on the other side, the teleporter, its tall chambers empty. Both were scorched, blackened by fire and soot. It was strange seeing these things, exhibited now as pieces of evidence. They were obviously trying to learn from the devices.

Further down the hall, another lab caught his eye. A man was sitting in a large chair, wearing what Tim recognised as a reader. However it was different – it had goggles and earmuffs, like a headset from some kind of virtual-reality game. Scientists in lab coats were taking notes and measurements. On the other side of the room, behind a partition, another man was wearing sticky pads on his temples, countless wires flowing from his head like long, dreadlocked hair. Tim watched in awe, ignoring the fact that Eisenstone and Harriet had rounded the corner out of sight. He felt a slight static throb coming from the window – it literally made his skin tingle. Some force, some incredible power, was being tested. There was a high-pitched hum, a weird digital sound that—

'Electromagnetic pulses.' An American voice came from behind, followed by a popping sound. Tim turned to see Fredric Wilde was by his side, also staring into the large lab. He was chewing bubblegum – it smelled of sweet strawberry. 'That's what you can feel.'

'What are they doing?' Tim asked.

'They are experimenting with something called a mind board. It *apparently* allows you to see the world through another person's eyes and, I've heard, even to take control of a person completely.'

This was obviously a prototype of what Harriet had described – a device similar to the one the Mind Surfer might be using. 'Does it work?'

'Of course not,' Fredric said. 'I ain't holding my breath on this particular project. Pie in the sky kinda thing.'

'Why does this organisation need such a machine?' Tim asked, having not completely understood Eisenstone's explanation of what they did.

'They spend billions of pounds creating brilliant things so that when the rest of the world catches up, we can be best protected. That's what they say, at least.'

'Protected?'

'TRAD was originally established to research weaponry. In an arms race, you need to have the biggest gun. But nowadays, with nanotechnology, quantum physics, a vast wealth of undiscovered potential, it's essential that they understand these things before they can be used against us. It's the agency's job to be one step ahead, at the cutting edge.'

'Right,' Tim said, looking at the warped reflection on the bulb of the reader. 'And what's your job?'

'I'm an entrepreneur ... a businessman. I sell computer parts, gadgets – got a few ventures online. I dabble in all sorts.'

'And you're allowed in here?' Tim asked, remembering this was a top-secret organisation.

'It's amazing the places you can go when you have enough money. Recently your fine government cut TRAD's funding almost clean in half, so they turned to the private sector for help. People like me, we're keeping this place afloat.'

'I see.'

'Tim,' Fredric said, lowering his voice slightly. 'I think I should be honest. TRAD has quite an extensive file on you and, when I heard who was in Harriet's office, I came to see you specifically.'

'Why?'

'I understand you very much enjoyed experimenting with Eisen*stone*'s technology.' The way he pronounced Eisenstone made Tim smile. 'Well, I have created something that surpasses it in virtually every way. I would like you to come to my facility and see it.'

'Yeah?' Tim felt a familiar rush of curiosity, wondering what on earth could be better than the imagination box.

'Yes, and I'd strongly advise you to agree.'

'Why is that?'

'Firstly, because it'll be the most fun you've *ever* had,' Fredric said, turning to face him properly for the first time. 'But mainly cos I think I know who *really* stole your imagination box . . .'

'Tim.' Eisenstone was striding back towards him. Harriet was waiting at the end of the long corridor – she looked down at her watch. 'Come on.'

'I'll be in contact. You mustn't utter a word of this to them,' Fredric whispered. He then turned and wandered off down the hall.

Harriet showed Tim and the professor into a dimly lit, spacious room, with an entire wall covered in flat-screen monitors. On the large one, in the centre, was some paused CCTV footage. It cast bright, bluish light on Harriet and Eisenstone – white squares in their eyes. Tim kept repeating, in his head, what Fredric had said. If it was true, if he knew where the box was, why couldn't he just tell Harriet?

'This is Glassbridge Mall.' Harriet pointed the remote. 'Yesterday afternoon.'

They watched the bird's-eye view of the busy centre – the silent, grainy video showed countless people walking between the shops.

'And here *you* come, Tim,' she added.

At the bottom of the image a black shape appeared, weaving between the shoppers, running at a rate of knots. Although the memory was a little blurry, the footage of him sprinting headlong straight into the large pane was as clear as the glass itself.

'Ouch,' Phil said. 'Might I ask, Timothy, why did you not stop?'

'I thought the door was open,' Tim said.

'Alas, the menace of transparency.'

The video showed Tim fall to the ground, sprawled out on his back. Then, as he'd suspected from his cobbled memories, the lollipop lady appeared. She walked directly up to him, crouched over his bag, and then stepped away with something bulging under her jacket. Harriet zoomed in on her face, which was pixelated beyond recognition. Tim squinted.

'*This* is who stole your imagination box,' Harriet said, turning. 'A forty-year-old lollipop lady named Grace Paulson, with no criminal record and no identifiable ties with any foreign or domestic organisation that might have an interest in such things.'

'So, indeed,' Eisenstone said, peering through his glasses, 'why *did* she steal it?'

'That, George, might be a little harder to determine,' Harriet added, lifting a folder.

'Why is that?' Tim asked.

'Because she's dead.'

Chapter 6

On the drive home Tim felt a squeeze of anxiety in his chest from the information. This was serious. He couldn't help but picture the woman's face – the blank expression she'd had when she demanded he hand over the imagination box. Initially he had been angry with her – annoyed that she'd chased and stolen from him – but now, realising she must be part of something far larger, he felt sorry for her.

It had turned out that the lollipop lady died the day after the theft, in a car crash – to an outside eye, little more than a tragic accident. But Harriet said she suspected it 'wasn't quite that simple'.

The whole way back, Eisenstone barely talked. Tim still got the impression, although he never said it, that the professor was profoundly disappointed with him.

Once again, he felt *determined* to find the box.

On that thought, after a particularly long silence, Tim said, 'What did you think of that Fredric guy?'

The professor shrugged. 'I think … well, I think it's a shame that such an important organisation has to, to rely on private funding,' he said.

To Tim, Fredric was exciting and seemed somehow cool. Eisenstone, on the other hand, had become quite reserved since last summer. Tim then recalled again what Fredric had said by that window. Not so much the bit about knowing who 'really' stole his imagination box, but the other thing. The part about having the most fun he'd ever had. Oh, now *that* was a bold statement.

Harriet had explained that a surveillance van would be parked outside the Dawn Star Hotel to keep close watch on him – he pictured the agents inside with cameras, recorders, microphones and the like. She said the fact that the thief or thieves – whoever he, she or they were – would likely be returning, as soon as they realised the imagination box was useless without the reader, was a good thing. It meant they had an opportunity to catch them. But it didn't exactly make Tim feel more secure about the whole situation.

The professor dropped him off at about 6 p.m. Tim pushed round the revolving door and, as he passed through the lobby, he looked at a few Dawn Star guests milling about, some queuing to check in, others sipping coffee. One, in particular, sitting on the sofa by the window, was wearing a long black coat and some large round sunglasses. She had short auburn hair, which was flattened by a tight woollen hat. Assuming she was one of TRAD's agents, Tim ignored her. Harriet had told him that they would 'blend in' and, to help them keep an eye on comings and goings at the hotel, he shouldn't draw any attention to them.

So he went straight up to his room, where he closed his curtains and weaved through some of the clutter that was *still* there, to get to his bed. Elisa had assured him it'd only be for a few days. In fact, it had been weeks now. Tim needed his own space more than ever – he felt trapped, scared, guilty and frustrated all at the same time. He slumped on to his mattress.

'There has been a great deal of deliberation and I have finally reached a conclusion,' Phil announced. 'My favourite film is *Jaws*.'

'Yeah?' Tim turned on to his side, watching the monkey pace along his bedside cabinet. 'Why is that?' Chatting to Phil usually comforted him.

'Primarily because it features a great white shark. Big bitey fish – just wonderful. They might be my favourite animal.'

'You said bears were your favourite.'

'Yes, last week. But *this week*, I must confess, sharks have been formally promoted.'

'They are good.'

'Timothy, you know they can breed donkeys with horses, and lions and tigers make ligers? And, of course, there's the famous pigosaurus rex.'

'Some of those are true.'

'Do you think scientists will ever be able to make a bear-shark splice?'

'I ... I doubt it. They are very different species. Plus, why would they want to?'

'I would pay dollar from the highest shelf for such a sight.'

Tim's phone rang loudly next to Phil, who leapt away, terrified. 'Sugar plum turnips,' he gasped, holding his tiny chest.

It was Elisa, calling Tim upstairs for dinner. Chris had just returned from a business trip so she had got some food from the Dawn Star kitchen: peppery, crackle-topped pork with mash and a stack of honey-roast carrots. He ate as much as he could, but wasn't feeling particularly hungry.

At the table, Tim tried to speak with Elisa about the theft of the box and about his visit to TRAD.

'There was this guy, Fredric,' Tim said. 'He invited me to his "facility".'

'Mmhmmm.' Elisa was washing a plate at the sink.

'He also said . . . he said something about . . . he said he knows who *really* stole the imagination box. And, weirdly, he said I couldn't tell anyone at TRAD. What do you think I should do?'

Elisa's phone buzzed on the draining board. 'Sorry,

Tim.' She locked the mobile, then turned. 'What were you saying?'

It seemed as though she wasn't in the mood for chatting. 'Never mind,' Tim sighed.

Almost exactly the same thing happened when he struck up a similar conversation with Chris. He was on the sofa typing away on his laptop, with his IcoRama on his thigh and his tablet perched on a cushion by his side. Again, he seemed so engrossed in his work – still wearing his suit, his tie loosened, the glowing screens all staring back at him.

'Hello?' Tim said, glancing between them. 'Am I invisible now?'

'Sure,' Chris muttered. 'Whatever you want.'

This was by no means the first occasion Elisa and Chris had been preoccupied. However, today they seemed especially distracted. Perhaps it was the added stress of the ongoing refurbishment, Tim wondered. That would explain Elisa, but Chris, when he was home at least, usually found some time for Tim.

'Anyway, as I was saying...' he started, before realising there was no point. Their thoughts were elsewhere.

He rolled his eyes and made his way back downstairs – apparently Phil was the only one who'd listen. At his door, he looked along the hallway – ornate lamps were posted between each room. One at the far end was broken, darkening the window and fizzing as though a fly was trapped in the bulb.

Stepping inside, he called out to Phil and, when he couldn't see the monkey, peered round the edge of some boxes as—

A shadow moved – a person was there. In his room.

Tim saw the whites of her eyes flash as she lurched forwards, grabbing him and slamming a hand across his mouth. There wasn't time to shout.

It was the woman from the lobby. Her fingers were cold, one palm pressed against Tim's neck, the other holding his jaw shut. She was so close he could smell her vanilla perfume and see the slight gloss of her lipstick. Standing together in his room, there was a moment of silence in which Tim realised he wasn't in immediate danger.

The woman's grip loosened and she lifted her index

finger to her lips, nodding a few times before she gently pulled her remaining hand away.

Still frozen, Tim didn't make a sound. Then she held up a piece of paper with a message written on it: *Don't talk, ears everywhere.*

Tim nodded as she wrote something else on the crumpled sheet. *Can you put some music on?*

Clicking his laptop on from standby, Tim did as she said, turning it up a few notches when she pointed to the ceiling. Although his heart was racing, he was more wary than scared, curious enough to hear her out.

'Where's Phil?' he whispered.

With a slight tilt of her head, she gestured to his top drawer. Tim opened it. Inside, the monkey was Sellotaped to his tiny little bed, his mouth stuck shut. His angry eyes were glaring, rolling around.

'What's going on?' Tim said.

'Shh!' She stepped closer. 'Sorry, but this was necessary.' She spoke in tight, breathy whispers, over the background music – which was some of Phil's jazzy swing. 'Listen, there isn't much time.'

'Hang on.' Tim squinted. He recognised her. 'I know you. You're ... you're from TV. From the news.'

'Yes.' She removed her woollen hat to reveal short, chop-cut, reddish hair. 'Samantha Locke. Sorry, we can do small talk another time, I—'

'Why have you broken into my room?' Tim said. 'This isn't OK.'

'I'm sorry to startle you, but we need to be discreet. Basically, what you need to know ... I have hacked into TRAD's files. I've read about what happened with your box.'

'Right.'

'It's ... it's a long story. Have ... have you heard of the Mind Surfer?'

Although unsure if sharing information with this intruder was a good idea, Tim figured she might have some details about the whereabouts of his missing device.

'I ... actually, yes,' he said. 'I have.'

'Good. I've been trying to get something concrete. But my boss, he says someone controlling people's thoughts is, to put it politely, nonsense.'

'OK ...'

'It's all linked. There are files on Crowfield House, on you and ... somehow ... it's all—'

'What are you talking about? You could have just phoned or sent me an email, like a normal person.'

'No, they're *everywhere*. Don't you understand?'

'Understand what?'

'My husband, he ...' Samantha was visibly overwhelmed. 'He was trying to prove that the Mind Surfer was real and, well, it cost him his life.'

'Like the lollipop lady ...' Tim said, almost to himself.

'She's dead?'

'Yes.'

'My God.'

'So, she *was* being controlled?'

'That's right, and when she'd served her purpose, she was silenced. That's what the Mind Surfer does. No loose ends.'

Tim swallowed, the trumpets loud from his speakers. 'But ... why?'

Reacting to a sound, she stepped to the window

and pulled the edge of the curtain across. 'Right, they're coming.' She strode back. 'All the files from TRAD's database, it's all connected and … and it all links back to you. The theft of your imagination box, Crowfield House, the Mind Surfer. I don't know how or why, but, Tim, it's all about *you*.'

There was a banging on the door. Samantha seemed to relax, as though there was no point in being secretive any more. 'Don't trust *any* of them. There will come a time when you run out of answers. When that happens, find me.'

She dropped a business card on his bedside cabinet, then opened the door.

Two tall men, dressed in black suits with curly-wire earpieces, grabbed her by the arms.

'Samantha Locke,' one of them said. 'Still sniffing around I see.'

The TRAD agents told Tim to stay in his room and then escorted her out of the building. Once they were gone, he perched on his bed and opened his drawer.

'The *audacity*,' Phil gasped, as Tim tugged the

tape away from his mouth. 'I must say, Timothy, that Samantha woman is most rude.'

Before Tim could process what she had told him, his mobile vibrated along his desk.

It was Dee. 'Hi,' Tim said, noticing how shocked he still sounded.

'You all right?' she asked. 'What's going on?'

'Something ... weird. I think it's best if we speak in person. Can you come round?'

Living just across town, Dee arrived fairly quickly. Tim then explained what had happened, from start to finish.

Dee laughed when he'd finished. 'Wow,' she said, sitting cross-legged on his bed. 'And this TRAD lot, you say it's one of the most advanced espionage agencies in the world?'

'Yes.'

'I have never heard of them.'

'*Exactly*,' Tim said.

'And they're here now?' She gestured around the room. 'Watching the hotel?'

'Yes.'

'And what do you think this "amazing" thing is at Fredric's facility?'

'I dunno,' Tim said. 'But when I go, I want you to come too.'

'You do get yourself in some strange situations.'

'Alas,' Phil put in, 'the common denominator does seem to be *you*, Timothy.'

'I didn't want this to happen.'

'You sure?' Dee asked. 'Hey, as whoever stole your imagination box probably killed their pawn, the lollipop lady, do you think that they'll kill *you* too when they're finished?' Her voice flashed with what sounded like excitement.

Tim frowned. 'Well *now* I do.'

'Seems like it's out of your hands, so best of luck with that. How far are you on Squirrel Boarder? It is super fun town.'

'Barely played it.'

'You know, I actually lost this earlier.' Dee pulled her mobile from her pocket. 'Mum was quite upset – even though she says I'm on it too much.'

'Where was it?' The normality of this conversation

felt weird for Tim, but was quite typical for Dee. Nothing seemed to faze her.

'In the park, on a bench. Luckily, I had phone finder installed, thank goodness.'

'Phone finder?'

'That app where you can use maps online to find it, if you leave it on the bus, or on the train or, say, in the park.'

Tim picked up the reader hat and turned it over so the small white letters, TIB, stared back at him. 'Sugar plum turnips indeed,' he said, his mind clicking into place.

He pulled the reader on to his head and swooped to his laptop. The monkey scurried along the carpet behind him, jumped on to the arm of the swivel chair and then on to the desk, spinning as he landed.

'What are we up to now?' Phil asked. 'Shark attack videos on YouTube? Well, good heavens, why not?'

'No. Do you remember at Crowfield House when I made those robo-bees appear in the imagination box?'

'Fondly.'

'I did it from the basement, right? I was a long

way away from the device itself. I can imagine things remotely.'

'You have my attention, Timothy – continue.'

'Well, what if I created a tracking device? Something that would appear inside the box, and transmit its location. Then we'd know where it was.'

'Yes, I am following. But, pray tell, why would you do this?'

'A, I promised Eisenstone I would get the box back safely, and B, whoever did this – they're murderers. We need to know who they are. Finding out *where* the box is, that's *surely* a start. It'll lead us right to this Mind Surfer person. Then we can tell TRAD, and they can go and arrest the culprits. Done. Home in time for supper.'

'Then you can get the imagination box back,' Dee said.

'Yes.'

'And create fine presents for me?' Phil added.

'Maybe.'

'A miniature motor-bicycle? Maybe one that hovers? Would that not just be the most *fabulous* thing?'

'And what about Samantha Locke?' Dee asked.

'I submit we put her in the thoroughly suspicious category,' Phil said. 'Sellotaping a defenceless little monkey? Frankly outrageous.'

'I dunno. First things first . . .' Wearing the reader, Tim closed his eyes and imagined a tracking device. After a few moments, he nodded. 'There, it's done. Now, if we just install the finder app on the ol' computer, we can get a location.'

'Your jib, Timothy, I do appreciate the manner in which it has been cut. Fine work.'

'Not just a pretty face . . .'

Tim clicked on his laptop, downloaded the software and entered the details of his freshly cooked tracking device into the appropriate boxes. He had imagined it would behave just like a phone, sending its location straight to the computer. When the loading bar sped across the bottom of the screen and a new window popped open with a map, he realised it was working.

Dee came and stood behind him, leaning over.

'Look,' Tim said. Phil scuttled on to the laptop's

keyboard, kneeling on the space bar and staring up. 'It's triangulating it with satellites.'

'Triangulating,' Phil repeated in a fascinated monotone. 'What is this?'

'Like ... finding it, or whatever ... right, it's finished.'

The screen flashed and the map, which had been an image of the whole of Great Britain, expanded as they zoomed in. Tim felt proud and excited as it magnified further and further until it arrived on a street in London. The small blue dot, indicating the imagination box's location, was slowly pulsing on the corner of a road.

'Where is that?' Dee asked.

'Somewhere in London. It's at ...' Tim scrolled out a little, getting a wider look at the map, growing desperate to know exactly where the stolen device was. 'It's at ... the Diamond Building?'

'Isn't that ...?'

'Yes,' Tim said, frowning, confused. 'That's TRAD's headquarters.'

Chapter 7

The next morning, Fredric rang Tim, as he said he would, and invited him to his office in London. The latest revelation meant that he jumped at the chance – Tim was curious to hear Fredric's view on the situation. However, as over the past couple of days everyone had been telling him he couldn't trust anyone else, Tim said he wanted Dee to come too.

'Sure,' Fredric said. 'The more the merrier, as you guys might say.'

Tim had felt totally trapped by his discovery that the imagination box was at the Diamond Building. Was someone at TRAD responsible for all of this? Was this what Samantha had meant when she said he shouldn't trust any of them? He'd stayed awake most of the night, unsure who to tell, unsure what to do. Had Eisenstone unwittingly walked him directly into the hands of those who stole the box?

Elisa gave swift approval for his trip to see Fredric. In fact, she was typing away at reception and barely looked up.

'Yes,' she'd said, waving her hand. 'That sounds fine.'

It had surprised Tim how little she was bothered about all this recent trouble – she didn't seem to care about TRAD's agents crawling all over the hotel. He assumed again that she was just extra busy with work. However, her increased apathy, although perhaps marginally preferable to disappointment, did fill him with an odd sadness.

Having popped home to grab some more clothes after staying the night, Dee arrived ten minutes before they were due to leave.

'So, what exactly is the plan?' she asked as she strode into his room, unravelling her scarf and perching herself on the edge of the bed. Without another word, she pulled her mobile from her pocket and looked down at it.

'We've got to go speak with Fredric Wilde.'

'Why? Do you just want to see his "super-duper exciting" facility?'

'No . . . I mean, maybe a bit. Fredric said he knows something – he can help.'

Again, Tim remembered Eisenstone's stoic disappointment – now tangled in this web, he knew he had to put right an ever-growing list of wrongs.

'So, essentially,' Dee said with a deep breath, 'to find your box, we've got to stop an unknown serial killer, one that possibly works for a secret, powerful government organisation? And they might be controlling people's minds too?'

'That's it.'

'Let me just finish this level.'

Tim rolled his eyes, but remained patient. He peered down – she was nearing quite a high score on Squirrel Boarder. Phil too, took an interest in the screen.

'What is the purpose of this game?' the monkey asked, glancing between Dee's face and the IcoRama.

'You've got to snowboard down the hill, avoid the spikes and not let the robot penguins catch you.'

'I find this scenario quite unlikely.'

'If you land three jumps in a row, you get an EMP grenade,' Dee added.

'What, pray tell, is an EMP grenade?' Phil asked.

'Electromagnetic pulse,' Dee said. 'It disables electronic devices.'

'Such as malevolent, cybernetic penguins?' the monkey said.

'Exactly.' Dee finished, with three stars, locked her phone, then sat up straight. 'OK, Captain Tim, what were you saying?'

'We've got to—'

'Oh yeah, that. Will it take long?' she asked. 'I have to cut the grass and sort the shed at home, to milk some cash out of Mum. You know that outrageously cool leather jacket I showed you? Well I've got to *save up* for it, like a normal person ... thanks to *someone's* reckless behaviour.'

'Then help me get the box back, expose the Mind Surfer, and fix this.'

'Timothy has promised to provide me with a miniature motor-bicycle, so I am sure he would be happy to create any of your desires,' Phil added.

Dee nodded at the monkey, then turned back to Tim. 'No sarcastic, superior comments about materialism,' she said, pointing. 'No resistance – you make me *anything* I want?'

'Yes, fine, deal,' Tim said.

'All right.' She stood. 'I'm in.'

Fredric sent an incredibly posh, stretched car to collect them – there were TVs and even a fridge in the back. His office was on the twenty-ninth floor of a tall, cube-shaped building with 'Wilde Tech' written in a fun, almost childish font over the door. Inside, the carpets were bright primary colours – yellows and reds. All the furniture was modern, ergonomic – curved glass tables and even beanbags in some of the conference rooms. It seemed a pretty cool place to work.

Upstairs Tim saw the vast, expansive view of London. A trio of pigeons, black against the clouds, flew across the sky. Below, far away, traffic gently flowed – commuters were mere dots.

'My word,' Phil said, leaping out and running up one of the frames. 'What a fine vista.'

'Thanks, man,' Fredric said, leaning by the glass.

The walls were decorated with various pieces of art and a couple of photographs mounted on canvas. One painting was a red Chinese-style dragon, with the words 'On the shoulders of giants' written beneath. Tim didn't really know what it meant.

On the opposite wall was a wide photograph of a sleek sports car.

'The Firestone Turbo,' Fredric said, noticing Tim's gaze. He stepped to the framed image. 'I have quite a collection of cars myself, but they only made three of these bad boys.' He sighed. 'It's funny how the one thing you can't buy is the one thing you want most.'

'Your business,' Dee said, strolling along the floor-to-ceiling window, 'seems to make lots of money.' She gestured at the expensive decor.

'We got a lot of fingers in a lot of pies.' Fredric nodded. 'And many of those pies are filled with tons of dough.' He perched himself on the edge of his long, polished desk. 'Gum?' he asked, holding out a light pink packet. Dee took some.

Fredric was wearing a thin green hoodie, jeans and trainers – all very casual except for, Tim noticed, the glistening watch that he saw when he rolled up his sleeve.

'I … I got something I want to tell you guys,' Fredric said. 'But … I mean, this has got to stay absolutely confidential. This is like a super-big deal – you've got to promise to keep it secret.'

'All right.' Tim was getting pretty used to this kind of thing.

'And Phil, Dee, you must not repeat this to a soul.'

'Heavens,' the monkey sighed, 'who would believe me anyhow?'

Dee gestured a zip across her mouth.

'Good. Now, how best to put this … It's about TRAD,' he went on. 'I've been associated with the agency a while now and every time I visit the Diamond Building I notice there are loads of places I'm not allowed to go. The only person who has ultimate clearance is Harriet Goffe, otherwise it's secrets at every turn. I understand discretion, but this is another level. Anyway, to cut a long story short ... I've done some digging and I *think* the people who stole your imagination box might work for TRAD.'

Tim looked to the floor and considered for a moment the best response. Of course, he'd been wondering as much himself. 'What ... what makes you think that?' He tested the water.

'It's a hunch, man.' Fredric shrugged. 'Those guys ... they are shadier than the night. They operate above the law. I think they killed that lollipop lady to cover it up. Hell, the box might even be *at* the Diamond Building. We just need to find out why, and then find a way to prove it.'

Tim saw that Fredric was stressed. He'd seen that expression on Elisa's face countless times – he was being worn thin. Fredric stepped away from the desk and walked silently to the window, where he placed his hand on the frame, and hung his head. Tim knew that Fredric was absolutely right to be suspicious of TRAD and now that they both wanted the same thing – to find his box and expose the culprits – he decided to trust him.

Dee and Tim made eye contact and she gave him a quick nod.

'You're right,' Tim said.

Fredric turned. 'About what?'

'The box *is* at the Diamond Building.'

'How … how do you know?'

'I can show you.' Tim stood and stepped round to the computer. True to his word, he loaded the map – the blue dot, almost breathing, sat in the middle of the square that marked the Diamond Building. Fredric leant over, clearly impressed.

'A tracking device,' he said. 'That is *super* clever, man.'

'There's more,' Tim went on. 'A woman, from TV, Samantha Locke … she broke into my room.'

'Yeah, TRAD has arrested her but they'll let her go in good time. Too high-profile.'

'She … she told me that it was all connected, that I shouldn't trust them.'

'Hmm.' Fredric lifted his eyebrows and pointed to his computer. 'That sounds like reasonable advice to me. But she was probably just looking for a story – wouldn't tell her too much if I were you.'

'So ... what's the next move?'

'Well,' Fredric said, standing up straight, tapping the wood with his knuckle. 'If the culprits are here in London, perhaps it would be best if we weren't. I wanna take you guys somewhere *awesome*.'

Fredric reached inside his pocket and removed a small plastic key ring, the kind used to lock cars remotely. Then he strode towards a wall on the far side of the office. As he got close to it, he clicked the button and the bricks parted in the middle with a loud hiss, revealing a secret room.

After exchanging a short glance, they followed. The space was small and lit like a hospital ward. There was nothing inside apart from four large red circles painted on the floor and four waist-high plinths in the centre of the room. On the middle of each of the small stands was a light blue sphere, about the size of a golf ball.

'Gate on,' Fredric said, stepping on to one of the marks. The spheres, responding to his voice, began to float above their holders. This was some expensive, high-tech stuff – Tim was impressed.

'What is this?' Dee asked, staring at one of the levitating balls, her mouth open in wonder.

'It's a quantum particle transmitting ... something or other.' Fredric waved his hand. 'I forget the technical name. It's a teleporter, essentially.'

Tim was wary of the technology, having seen Clarice Crowfield destroyed in such a machine. 'Does ... does it work?'

'Course it works,' Fredric said, noticing Tim's nerves. 'This is Wilde Tech ... this wasn't built by some mad scientist in a secret, gloomy lab. Although Professor Whitelock's work certainly contributed to this latest design.'

'Where does it go?' Tim asked.

'My underground complex that I mentioned before. It's great – you're gonna love it. Very simple,' he said, holding one of the floating blue balls. 'You press the button on the side and every particle you're made of – blood, bone, skin – will be completely destroyed, removed, as it were, from the universe. You'll then be recreated perfectly at the other end. Isn't the future beautiful?'

'Does it hurt?' Dee asked – Tim could tell she was itching to have a go, despite that gruesome explanation of the process.

'Not even slightly.'

'And it's completely safe?' Tim added, his heart picking up a little.

'Nothing is *completely* safe, Tim.'

'I'm not sure,' he said, stepping into another circle.

'Fine.' Fredric shrugged, blowing a pink bubble which popped loudly. 'But I'm going.'

And, with a click and the shortest whipping sound, Fredric was gone. The blue sphere floated back down on to the platform.

Dee was smiling. 'Maybe,' Tim said, 'we shouldn't—'

But before he could finish, Dee had pressed hers and disappeared in a blink, the faintest suggestion of dust where she'd been.

Now alone with Phil in his top pocket, Tim sighed.

'I respect your reluctance,' the monkey said.

'Knowing when to say no is a crucial trait to have.' Tim reached out and placed his hand on the hovering sphere. 'Or just ignore me,' Phil added, 'that is fine too.'

Tim swallowed his fear and rubbed his thumb down the cool metal until he found the small recessed switch. Oddly, he closed his eyes and even felt tempted to hold his nose as though he was about to plunge into water. 'Ready?'

'No.'

'Shall I do it?'

'I suggest not.'

'I think I'm going to.'

'Then why ask?'

Sucking in a breath, Tim had one last look at the bright room and pressed the button.

There was nothing.

But then there was a gasp and Tim opened his eyes. His brand-new eyes. In his hand was a small sphere, just like the last, only this one was orange. He let go of it and, like its counterpart, it slowly floated down on to its holder. Now he was standing in a large, modern laboratory – strip lights ran the length of the room and, although he couldn't put his finger on why, he felt as though they were many miles away. Everything was different. Foreign. A whirring sound in his ears, the kind you hear when you yawn, faded to complete silence.

'Oh no ... *no*,' Fredric said, stepping round in front of Tim. 'Don't move, don't move an inch. Neither of you.'

'What?' Tim glared, tensing all his muscles. 'What is it?'

He saw Dee – she had her hand over her mouth and concern in her eyes.

'Oh my God.' Fredric looked terrified. 'I am so sorry ...'

'What? What's going on?'

'I too am keen to know,' Phil said from Tim's pocket, also frozen rigid.

'Please don't panic. I'll get a doctor – they might be able to fix this.'

'Fix what? *Might?*' Tim, despite the advice, was beginning to panic.

Fredric rubbed his hand through his short hair, then placed the back of it against his lips. 'Are you familiar with the movie *The Fly*? It's about a scientist experimenting with a teleporter and … well … he accidently creates a splice between himself and an insect. A man-bug hybrid. I didn't remember to warn you to go through alone … and now …'

'Oh *goodness gracious*,' Phil said.

'No …' Tim shook his head, feeling as though he was about to vomit. '*No*.'

Fredric's eyes gradually grew moist with sadness … no … not sadness. Something else. He began to … to smile and, after a second or two, let out a deep laugh. He clutched his stomach and swung his head back, revelling in the moment. Dee, too, was banging a nearby table as she guffawed away.

'Ha ha,' he said, waving an arm. 'You're both fine. We're just kidding.'

'Oh, ah … ha … ha ha.' Tim faked a gentle laugh. 'Very … very good.'

'I personally did not enjoy that joke,' Phil said, leaping from Tim's pocket and on to a desk. He quickly checked his body, running his tiny hands over fur.

'Chill out, monkey man,' Fredric said. 'The

teleporter is safe. Now, welcome to *my* playground.'

They walked through a pair of automatic doors and down a long corridor. 'Where are we?' Dee asked.

'This is one of TRAD's old research facilities.' Fredric looked over his shoulder as he continued forwards. 'I'm leasing it from them, but will buy it soon enough.' A man in a lab coat passed them in the hall – Fredric gave him a high five. 'We run a skeleton staff here – me and two technicians. That's it.'

Dee and Tim walked quickly to keep up until they were in a new area. It had a low ceiling and a small raised space at the end, hosting a semicircular desk filled with computers and screens. Lights glimmered and faded on and off at every workstation – red, green, blue, white. Complex dials and equipment covered all surfaces and walls. It looked like a music mixing station Tim'd seen on TV. On the wall opposite was a large window. Outside it was pitch black – not even a single star in sight. Again, Tim felt as though they were in another world.

'How far have we come?' Tim asked, assuming they were in a different time zone.

'Leaps and bounds, man,' Fredric said, hitting a light switch. 'Leaps and bounds.'

Tim realised that the window wasn't looking outside, but rather into another room, which lit up below them. It was huge, like an aircraft hangar. Only much bigger.

'Whoa,' Dee said, peering through – she looked as fascinated as Tim felt.

Fredric stood on a square on the floor and waved them over. 'Come on.'

As they stepped on to the platform, it hissed and descended quick enough to make Tim sway to keep his balance – Dee grabbed his arm. They arrived in a narrow, dim corridor and approached an unusually old-fashioned door – rectangular wooden panels and a brass handle, carved to look like the head of a dragon – that opened with a slight gust of air from the change in pressure. A gasp.

The cool expanse could be felt; the sheer space in front of them was somehow unmistakable by the deep silence. Fredric went in first, walking off across the vast, empty floor. Dee wandered in by his side.

Warily Tim followed, stepping along the smooth concrete. It was daunting, almost vertigo-inducing. He felt tiny, turning completely round as he followed Fredric and Dee, walking backwards, sideways, looking up at the tall, dark grey walls. There were discreet steel support beams that ran around the centre, like the ribs of some kind of gigantic, square, robotic whale. And behind was what had seemed a huge window but, as they got further and further away, it became tiny, no more than a postage stamp on a football field.

In the very middle of this grand space was a small plinth with a glass container on top. Tim hadn't even spotted it until they arrived.

'Where are we?' he finally asked.

Phil climbed on to his hand, then on to the edge of the small podium. Fredric smiled at the monkey, who arched his neck to take in what he was seeing.

'We are very deep underground, beneath the Nevada desert,' Fredric said. His voice sounded crisp, clean. Tim had suspected they'd travelled some distance, but not *this* far. Not to America. 'Up there is nothing but miles and miles of dry shrubby earth, scorched red rocks and eagles squawking high above. Just like the movies. I've got a private Learjet parked at the airfield too. Lovely thing – I'll show you later.'

Tim gazed up – directly above them, astonishingly high, was a round service hatch.

'*That* takes you to the surface,' Fredric added.

'What *is* this?' Dee said.

'You haven't realised?' he asked, pressing a small switch. 'I think they used to build airships in here. But now ... now it's something else entirely.'

Fredric pulled a device from atop the stone: a piece of metal that looked a little like a crown, only thin and black. It had a line of blue lights around the edge. He put it on his head – there was a quiet electric hiss, like a camera's flash warming up.

'How about now?' he said, lifting an eyebrow.

Tim walked a full circle around him, staring up at the distant ceiling, left and right to the walls, which seemed a mile apart.

'It's ...' he said, his mouth locked in an open smile. 'It's a giant imagination box.'

Chapter 8

Tim was utterly desperate to have a go. The idea that he could create things – huge things – right in front of his eyes was beyond exciting, beyond any of the words he knew.

'But, as you've probably noticed,' Fredric said, looking up towards the far end of the vast, expansive space, 'it's empty.'

'It doesn't work?' Tim's heart sank.

'Oh, it works. It is a straight remake of Eisenstone's prototype, taken from TRAD's blueprints, only larger. Better. This is how true advancements are made.'

'It must have taken *years* to build?' Dee said.

'No.' Fredric shook his head, pouting. 'Great lengths of time fall to the wayside when faced with will and money. I have both in excess. Besides, I'm not hindered by caution – I won't let risk stand in the way of progress.'

Tim assumed he was referring to Eisenstone and, to be fair, he was right. The professor was paranoid, at times almost paralysed by fear.

'So, why are *we* here?' Tim asked, although he suspected he already knew the answer.

'You know what the first question everyone at TRAD asked when they heard about Eisenstone's progress? Why, why can you, Timothy Hart, use the box?'

Tim had wondered this many times before. He remembered the countless instances Dee had tried . . . to no avail.

'Yeah,' she said. 'Why indeed.'

Fredric shrugged. 'I have a theory. I think it might be your capacity for original thought.'

'What does that mean?' Tim asked.

'Most people are restricted by what their elders tell them, by what they've seen, heard, smelled, *experienced*. There are no cave drawings of jumbo jets. There's no ancient Egyptian hieroglyph for the internet. Why?'

'Because those things didn't exist back then,' Dee said.

'Exactly. You need someone to have invented the wheel before you invent the car. Standing on the shoulders of giants . . . A good exercise is to imagine a new colour.'

'Easy,' Phil said, closing his eyes.

'Is it sort of bluish?' Tim asked.

'I . . . yes.'

'That's the thing,' Fredric added. 'Even if Tim, or anyone, *could* imagine a new colour, he'd never be able to describe it to anyone else – we've got no point of reference. I suspect some brains can do this, and others can't.'

'Can it be learned, do you think?' Dee asked.

'I'll be totally honest with you, I don't know. I have no idea why Tim can use it and no one else seems to be able to. But I *want* to know. I want to develop the technology. Make it accessible, commercial. That's why I've constructed this.'

'So you've not tested it yet?' Tim asked.

'No, but we've done a hell of a lot of theory. Eisenstone has probably explained it as best he can, but the truth is . . . even he doesn't understand it fully.'

'And *you* do?' Dee asked.

'No way,' Fredric said. 'But it's not *just* moving atoms in the right order, as he might have us believe. Physicists, man, they love being rigid with their rules.'

'He told me that nanomachines build the items, one molecule at a time,' Tim said.

'That's true to a point,' Fredric added. 'But let me ask you this . . . does space end?'

'What?' Dee frowned.

'When you look up at the stars at night, how far does it go? Either the universe has an edge, or it is infinite and goes on forever. Personally, I can't get my head around either one of those options. You see, if it is in fact infinite, that means everything that can happen, will happen and *has* happened. That means there are other worlds, just like this one. Somewhere the sea is green not blue, or where grass grows a fraction faster. Somewhere, a monkey has just randomly typed the complete works of Shakespeare.' He glanced at Phil. 'There is another you, another me, an infinite number of mes and yous. There's an infinite number of everything. Every conceivable combination of atomic matter exists.'

'O . . . K.' Tim nodded. 'What does that have to do with this technology?'

'Just on base theory, there are obvious deductions to be drawn. First and foremost, you can't make something from nothing. That fact's immovable. Like energy, it just transfers. This matter you're bringing into the world is coming from *somewhere*. Maybe it's not being created, but rather *borrowed* from an alternate reality, a parallel universe.'

'That's why Tim was able to get full marks on his schoolwork?' Dee said.

'Yeah.'

'So it *was* cheating,' she added.

'I'm afraid so – that stuff, it isn't in your mind, Tim. Put simply, you *might* have access to endless knowledge, infinite information. The human brain is the most complex, fascinating tool known to man. And this technology is unlocking it in new ways.'

Fredric slowly removed the black, crown-like reader from his head and placed it on Tim's. It was cold, metallic. Tim felt it run through the hair above his ears, tickling his scalp, sending goosebumps down his back and across his arms. It fit perfectly . . . It was small, made for a child.

'Made for you,' Fredric said, as though he'd read Tim's thought. 'I should be honest from the start here: it will take readings from your brain while we test it. Is that all right?'

'Yeah, whatever you say.' Tim was too eager to listen to the small print.

'I suggest we start with something simple, small.'

The more Tim thought about it, the more he realised he quite liked Fredric. A fine chap, as Phil might say. As such, Tim decided it only fair to give him a gift. He recalled the picture he'd seen in his office, making it as clear as he could in his head. Once it had settled, he nodded slightly as he did with his own reader. Somehow he could feel the image flow to the edges of his skull and transmit itself into the thin black crown.

There was a faint crackling, then a quick noise behind the plinth, as thin air was replaced with matter, and it was done. The object was there.

Fredric's brow lowered as he turned to see a Firestone Turbo sports car, its blood-red bonnet almost as reflective as a mirror, waiting patiently for him. Although he was facing away, Tim saw his ears rise a little. He was happy.

'Dee,' Tim said, facing her, 'lift up your arms.'

The coolest studded leather jacket Tim could imagine faded into existence around her. She stepped backwards, touching the material, speechless.

Without uttering a word, Fredric approached the vehicle. Leaning low he cupped a hand on the glass, peering inside at the supple leather interior, at the silver finish on the maroon dashboard and the twisted web of chrome spokes on the steering wheel. After a few moments, Fredric slowly grabbed the handle, as though he was reaching out to touch a wild animal.

'It's locked,' Tim said. 'It's an expensive car. I'm not just going to leave the doors open.'

Fredric turned round, his chin dangling in awe. Tim very much liked creating that response in people.

'Hold out your hand,' Tim said. 'And close your eyes.'

A set of keys fizzed instantly into existence a few centimetres above Fredric's palm, then fell into his grasp.

'Th-thank you,' he said, completely humbled by the present. 'Really, this ... *this* is what money can't buy.' Fredric's smile looked authentic, endearing.

There was a radio buzz, then a voice spoke high above them. 'Fredric, there's a call for you on the landline ...'

'All this technology and you're taking calls on the landline?' Dee said.

'I rarely use a cell phone. I don't want my day dictated by other people,' Fredric said. 'Besides, there's no signal down here anyway. Look, just stay put – we'll resume this shortly.'

Once he was gone, Tim looked around the empty

imagination space, then gestured Phil into his top pocket.

'Bit bare, isn't it?' Dee said. She then shouted, 'Hello,' towards the back wall. It echoed again and again, reminding Tim just how *massive* this place was.

Closing his eyes, he started to imagine – a moment later he lifted his shoulders and stepped on to a dirt path. When he looked again, he was guiding Dee through a wooded area: thin branches with freshly grown cherry blossom – soft pinks against light grey bark – were hanging over the track. He travelled slowly, brushing the backs of his hands along the sprouting ferns, which curled at his waist. Specks of floating seedlings danced in the air in front of them and a pair of absurdly colourful, *glowing* butterflies – yellow wings tipped with neon blue – flew in tight, jarring circles around one another. They heard birdsong, tweets overlapping, melodic and recognisable. The singing was halfway between human and animal, in the style of a barbershop quartet, and Tim knew they'd take requests.

The trees ended and a long expanse of flat concrete

quickly turned to mud. Then a layer of brand-new, golf-course standard grass appeared and stretched into the distance. His imagination escaped all around him, flourishing its way into the real world.

Leading Dee by the hand, Tim crossed the plain, turning to look back at the lush woodland behind them – he could smell the clear sap and fresh flowers, which grew thicker and more perfect even now. The floor beneath him turned to cobblestone and wide granite steps appeared as they walked higher and higher. Each new stair materialised just as his foot reached its surface. And, quicker than he expected, a daunting palace – a broad-shouldered castle – constructed itself from the ground up in a matter of moments. The building was gigantic, five storeys high, now six, and yet still it wasn't even halfway to the ceiling. The steel ribs above gradually disappeared behind a haze of clouds.

'Tim,' Dee whispered, her arms by her side, awestruck.

To their left a cool mist became a torrent of water, bursting from a cliff and flowing down its face. It turned into a busy, shallow river, weaving between brand-new rocks and instantly carving its way under the stone bridge they'd just crossed, creating a moat. The spray made a row of rainbows so vivid they looked like ribbons of paint.

They stepped into the castle as the walls flowered into view and candles popped into the world one by one. Phil, for once, was stunned into silence – he watched on from the top pocket. They travelled up a wide, spiral staircase and headed down the hall. The royal red carpet cushioned his feet. And then he paused, frowned, and smiled once again as circular patterns, like the Dawn Star's stepping stones, appeared on the floor beneath them. Laughing, they leapt from one swirl to the next, and Tim wondered whether turning the ground to real lava would be worth the risk.

Open doors appeared. A room to his right hosted a deep swimming pool, the walls decorated with Mayan-style pillars, covered with dried vines and tinted turquoise by the underwater lights. A room to his left housed a wall-sized flat-screen TV and every conceivable entertainment system, both old and new – box-fresh consoles next to classic arcade games, snooker tables next to pinball machines. The next room was a multistorey library, with books from floor to ceiling and one of those rolling ladders Tim had always wanted to try. Another was filled with easels, paints, pens, clay – a well-equipped studio with every medium available for him to enjoy. And, even beyond his view, his mind was furnishing this place with everything he'd ever wanted and much, much more.

As they ascended further into the palace, Tim smiled as he thought of the clutter in his bedroom. How minor a concern that now seemed.

On the roof he stepped to the edge, climbed up and tucked his legs between the cold stone uprights of the castle's battlements, sitting comfortably with his elbow on one. Phil scurried on to his lap, then on to the granite by his side, and Dee fit nicely in the next crenel. They stared across the vista, now a valley, and no one said a word. After a few moments, Tim realised it wasn't yet complete.

So he lifted his arm. 'And there was light,' he said, clicking his fingers.

A bright orange – as rich as a sunset against the Sahara – flooded everything around them.

To the left, Tim noticed Fredric striding across the plain. He then created an awesome spiral slide, which took them from the top of the castle, down to the ground where Fredric greeted them.

Turning around, gesturing at the space, he laughed. 'Tim ... this is *incredible* ... this place is ... it's beautiful.'

Things were still appearing inside, plants were sprouting at the base of the building – hedgerows and sculptures, water features and paths – as Tim's subconscious fully furnished the new world.

'That was Harriet on the phone,' Fredric said after expressing his astonishment. 'Somehow she's worked out that we're here. I think she wants you back at TRAD's HQ – which doesn't seem like the best idea.'

Tim sighed, remembering that outside these walls was the *real* world. Part of him wanted to just create a new imagination box in here and forget about the last. But then he recalled a *promise* he'd made to Eisenstone. He would get the box back.

'Fine,' Tim said. 'So what are we gonna do?'

'Something a little crazy and quite dangerous – we'll run over the plan in a moment. But first, let me show you something. Have you considered what you do if you make a mistake in here?'

'What do you mean?'

Fredric pulled a small black device from his pocket; it looked like a strange sort of gun, just with an extremely short barrel.

'Create something over there, anything . . . create a soccer ball. Sorry, a *football*.' He put on a poor English accent.

Without even looking at where he wanted it, Tim imagined a white leather ball – it fell on to the grass, bounced once, then rested still.

'Creation is only one side of the coin . . . should you wanna remove something from the world, you will need this.'

Turning on his heel, Fredric pointed the black

Chapter 9

Amid the ashen light of the moon, there was no sound at TRAD's headquarters besides the faint humming from some distant electronics. The room – all of the Diamond Building in fact – was asleep, at peace. On the wall a clock ticked – it was 9.32 p.m. A quick hissing pop gave way to a pair of figures – aptly clad as burglars in black – who appeared behind a partition.

'Uuuuhhh,' Dee whispered, shuddering from the teleport. 'It's so weird – makes me feel a little bit sick. Queasy town.'

'Shh.' Tim crouched, dragging her to the ground with him. He pocketed the orange teleportation sphere, which Fredric had hidden here, and then straightened his imagination-box beanie.

'Why are we crouching?' Dee wondered.

'I dunno.' They stood up straight.

Fredric had given them a small USB device, which he told them to plug into Harriet's personal computer.

'She's TRAD's director,' Fredric had said. 'Her computer has the highest clearance – it has access to *all* of TRAD's files. If anyone there knows about the box, about the Mind Surfer, the answers will be on her hard drive.'

He had also shown them on a map where they would arrive and explained their route in and out, highlighting where cameras and guards would be posted.

As they were on the thirty-fourth floor, they could see for miles. The night scene – lights peppered across a black canvas – stretched all the way to the horizon. To the right, a deep storm cloud was moving in, a few specks of rain appearing on the glass already and, in the distance, silent flashes of white were glowing in the sky.

'Come on,' Dee said, heading out of the room.

This was an evening of broken rules as, in order to be out this late, Dee had told her mother that she was staying at Tim's. And Tim, you guessed it, had told Elisa he was staying at Dee's. Fredric had said, 'Honesty will come later – they'll understand in the long run.'

They knew where they needed to go – up four storeys, down a long corridor, into Harriet's office and then on to her computer. Straight in. Straight out. That was the plan. They got to the end of the first hall without incident, avoiding the CCTV camera, which slowly shook its head from side to side. They took the steps two at a time, safe in the knowledge that there were no cameras and no security in the stairwell. On the landing they stood before a flat concrete wall with the number thirty-eight stamped in huge, faded white letters. This was the top floor of TRAD's HQ where some of the most senior members of staff worked – it was the brain of the beast.

Tim reached out and grabbed the door handle, clenching his teeth as he gently pulled it down, trying to stay silent. With the softest of clicks it opened on to the long corridor, bordered by internal windows – rows of offices and testing labs. Everything was still and grey, just the odd red dot from screens on standby.

'Right,' Tim said. 'Phil, let's go.'

The monkey, also dressed in black (tiny little hat, tiny little jacket – he'd even added two stripes of dark camo paint to his cheeks), leapt from Tim's pocket, climbed up a door frame, and clung to the long strip lights. He headed off down the hall above them, all the way to the corner – he could be their eyes and ears, high and small enough to avoid detection. Tim saw him freeze at the sight of something, then he came scurrying back.

'There's a guard up there,' Phil quietly announced. He fell to the carpet between them. 'Up there, around the corner. He has a gun.'

'What do you mean?' Tim whispered, lowering himself to the ground.

'I *mean* precisely what I said … he literally has *a gun*.'

'Why?' Tim gasped, fear arriving.

'To shoot intruders I imagine.' Dee squinted as though it was a silly question.

'This is altogether disheartening,' Phil said. 'I suggest a comprehensive and noble retreat.'

'No,' Dee whispered. 'As long as he doesn't see us, his gun is irrelevant. And even if he does, he won't shoot.'

'Won't he?!' Tim said.

'Probably not.' Dee shrugged. 'Come on, don't worry about it. Let's just be quick.'

'All right,' the monkey put in, scurrying up to Tim's pocket. 'But stealth is of paramount importance. Team Phil, we must tread lightly.'

Dee shuffled low to the ground, but Tim remained still. 'Wait,' he said. She looked over her shoulder.

'What is it?' she snapped.

'We're not called "Team Phil".'

'Oh, I am sorry,' the monkey whispered. 'Care to speculate what our team name is then?'

'I don't think we need one. But, if it's anything, it should be Team Tim,' he said. 'Alliteration.'

'Hmm,' Dee shook her head. 'Not so sure.'

'All of our names or none of them,' Phil suggested.

'Or our initials?'

'Team TPD,' Tim said.

'Suits me fine, sir.'

'Well, hang on,' Dee whispered. 'Why is my name last, that's—'

The guard at the end of the hall coughed.

'We can settle this later,' Tim said. 'Come on.'

Running, bent at the waist, they made it to the corner. Phil confirmed the man was pacing. Tim, lying on the floor, took a quick look. True enough, the security guard was walking the length of the next hallway ... at the end of which was Harriet Goffe's office.

'We'll have to time it perfectly,' Tim whispered.

They waited until he turned and wandered away, his back to them.

'Go, go, go.'

Now on all fours, they crawled along, getting inside the spacious office just as the armed man was turning at a noise he may or may not have heard. Tim pressed his back against the door, and silently closed it. He held his finger to his lips, staring at Dee as they waited. A few moments later, when they knew they were in the clear, they sprung into action.

Straight to the computer. Tim sat on the swivel chair and pulled the plastic lid off the USB stick Fredric had given him. The device, he had been told, had software pre-installed that would automatically download all of Harriet's emails and files.

Only now did Tim feel a real wave of panic. What were they doing? Spying on the boss of a secret government agency was just so illegal.

'This is properly naughty,' Tim said, almost to himself. 'You sure we should do it?'

Dee rolled her eyes, pushed him aside, snatched the USB stick and plugged it in herself.

The screen lit up. 'Enter Admin Password,' it read.

'Oh,' Tim said. He was strangely relieved. This meant they might not have to go through with the crime.

'I feel like we're missing something,' Dee said, looking around the office.

'Yes. A password.'

'No ... something else.' She scratched her head. 'Wait a second. There's something ... something not right.' She stepped towards the door.

Without another word, she left the room, crawling down the hall. Tim, not knowing where the guard was, quickly followed. He caught up with her a little way down the corridor, where she'd reached a maintenance cupboard and opened it up. She pulled her mobile phone from her pocket and used the torch on the back to look inside: a mop propped against the wall, the smell of bleach, a vacuum cleaner curled up in the corner. The bright light made shadows wobble and sway.

'Dee,' Tim hissed through his teeth.

'Hang on.' She stepped inside, ran her hand along the underside of a shelf at the back, then looked to the floor. She pushed a plastic container away, exposing a large cardboard box.

'*What* are you doing?'

'Look, look at this.'

Pulling back one of the flaps, she opened it. For

Tim, the moment took him back in time, reminiscing about the day he'd done something similar. Hidden in the plain cardboard, at the back of the maintenance cupboard, was his imagination box.

'There you are,' Phil said. 'You elusive little rascal.'

Tim fell to his knees and lifted the sleek, silver contraption on to his lap. 'Oh, I've missed you.' He stroked the reader hat on his head, feeling complete again. He couldn't wait to tell Eisenstone that he'd kept his promise, that he'd found the gadget. This was the sweetest of victories.

Looking back up, he saw Dee was smiling.

'How on *earth* did you know this was here?' Tim asked.

'I just had a feeling.'

'A feeling? Of all the rooms, all the floors, the thousands of possible places it could be hidden in this building, you had a *feeling* it was here, in this cupboard?'

'Went with my intuition,' she said. 'I mean, it felt weird, but I had a strong urge to look here. Do you never get that sort of thing – raw gut instinct? Plus, think about it – this is the closest possible hiding place to Goffe's office.'

'I … suppose,' Tim said, still astonished.

'Now you can imagine Harriet's password.'

'I could …' Tim added. 'Would it work?'

'Remember what Fredric said – infinite info? What about all those books in the castle's library? What about your homework?' Dee shrugged. 'What about all the components for your imagination box? You managed to create that. Imagine it written on a scrap of paper.'

They shuffled back to Harriet's office, timing their entry so the guard didn't see them. Inside, Tim placed the imagination box on the low coffee table in the corner of the room, closed his eyes, leant forwards and did his best to imagine what it might be like if he could conjure *pure unknowns* into the world.

Nodding to let Dee know he'd finished, Tim stood back. She opened the box and pulled out a fortune cookie.

'This is not what I ordered,' she whispered.

'Break it open.'

With a hollow crack she pulled the two sweet shells apart, a few crumbs sprinkled from her hands, and a small tail of thin paper curled: *SugarDan101*.

'Who's Dan?' Tim wondered.

'Just type it in.' Dee was eager.

Tim double-checked the spelling and keyed the password. He hesitated. 'You think this will—'

Dee leant over and struck enter. The screen flickered black, then the desktop appeared.

'Fiddlesticks and peppercorns,' Phil gasped. 'We're in. This does raise some potent philosophical questions.'

'Well,' Tim said. 'That *is* interesting.'

The window opened and he clicked the programme Fredric had installed on the USB stick – all emails and documents began downloading automatically. Outside there was a rumble of thunder and a whistling wind – the storm was closing in. Tim chewed his thumbnail as the loading bar filled from left to right across the bottom of the screen.

'Don't you want to . . . you know,' Dee said. 'Diddly doo, snooperoo?'

'What?'

'Have a read. Little nosey?' She clicked open Harriet's emails. 'Do a search.'

'For what?'

'Your name. See who was involved in the theft of the box. This computer has ultimate clearance – if TRAD *do* know anything, it'll be here.'

Tim did as she said, typing his name into the email search bar.

'Does this not feel like a huge invasion of her privacy?' Phil asked.

'Yes, but the imagination box was hidden in the cupboard near her office,' Dee said. 'This is called just cause.'

The download was at twenty-two per cent when an exchange of emails, in which Tim was mentioned, appeared on screen.

Fri, Feb 14, at 6:02 PM, Daniel Moore <d.moore@trad.com> wrote:

Harriet,
The job is complete – we ran into some

hiccups initially, he outran Subject 43 but we were able to deliver appropriate signals to Subject 44 and she behaved accordingly. Acquisition of device went to plan – Timothy Hart gave her a run for her money, but then he ended up unconscious (lol). There might be some CCTV footage to add to the loose ends. Awaiting further orders.

Dan x

Sat, Feb 15, at 1:15 PM, Harriet Goffe <h.goffe@trad.com> wrote:

Dan,

How far we've come in such a short time. There will be repercussions – George will bring Tim in. Discretion is crucial, this stays between us. Hold fire for now, I'll provide you with instructions in due course.

Harriet

Sat, Feb 15, at 1:16 PM, Daniel Moore
<d.moore@trad.com> wrote:

Harriet,
Should I be prepped for lethal
intervention?
Dan x

Sat, Feb 15, at 1:18 PM, Harriet Goffe
<h.goffe@trad.com> wrote:

Dan,
Absolutely. Move forwards with the
termination of Subject 44. Make it look
like an accident – car crash or the like.
Do it today.
Harriet

Sat, Feb 15, at 3:26 PM, Daniel Moore <d.moore@trad.com> wrote:

Harriet,

It's done. Paulson is toast. What's our next move?

Dan x

'Wow,' Tim whispered. 'It's them. They did it all. Harriet and this guy Daniel ...'

He read the final email:

Sat, Feb 15, at 4:00 PM, Harriet Goffe <h.goffe@trad.com> wrote:

Dan,

Your services shall be required in due course, for now, rest easy. I'll let you know what to do with the kid at a later date, but I expect – like all these frayed edges – our only option is, regrettably, termination.

Harriet

'What ... what do you think it means? "Termination"?' Tim whispered, although he reckoned he already knew.

Phil was standing, one foot propped on the edge of the keyboard, looking up at the screen. 'Do you *really* not know?'

'This email implies they intend to kill you, Tim,' Dee said. 'It is quite obvious.'

'I notice they are using Comic Sans,' Phil added, pointing up at the monitor.

'Yeah,' she hummed, leaning in. 'That's not professional at all. This ain't a poster for the village fête.'

'I suspect Arial would be more in keeping with the office environment,' Phil said. 'Although I am partial to Times New Roman.' The monkey turned around. 'What's your favourite font, Timothy?'

Tim had been listening to this exchange with his mouth locked open in astonishment. 'I think the noteworthy part of these emails is the bit where Harriet and Daniel discuss conspiracy and, you know, murder,' he said, slowly, doing his best not to be angry.

'Sor-ry,' Dee said.

'Yes, Timothy, we were just making conversation.'

'Look, never mind,' Tim said. 'Let's get this stuff together and get out.'

'I do wonder what Harriet, with all her authority, would have to gain from this,' Phil said. 'Is this all just a ploy to get your imagination box? Controlling people's minds? Perhaps a little over the top? They could have just asked.'

'Seems like part of something much bigger,' Tim said. 'Fredric said they operate above the law – this is probably one of many schemes.'

'We can find all that out later,' Dee added. 'We've got proof that Harriet and this Daniel bloke are wrong'uns. That's all that matters right now.'

The download bar had almost filled at the bottom of the screen – it was at eighty-nine per cent.

'Anyway, what is it?' Phil said, looking up from the desk. 'Your preferred font?'

'I haven't got a f—' There was a clunk outside the room. They all stopped – poised as statues. 'Be quiet,' Tim whispered.

Standing from the chair, he saw the progress on the download reach ninety-nine per cent. It paused, then tipped to one hundred. He pulled the memory stick from the computer. Now all that was left was to sneak out of this place and present the evidence to—

'What does that mean?' Phil said, pointing at the top of the emails.

'Which bit?'

'People copied in . . . g.eisenstone? Is this to infer *he* received these messages?'

Dee typed another search – emails containing her grandfather's name shot to the top of the list. The first one was entitled 'payment'. They read that Harriet had paid Professor Eisenstone a great sum of money for his 'silence concerning this sensitive matter'.

Tim's stomach turned. He noticed his hands were shaking. A wave of physical sickness made him sway – the idea that the professor might have lied triggered in him a feeling of hopeless confusion and terrible loneliness. It felt as though he was falling.

'Eisenstone . . . knew about this?'

'He's part of it?' Dee whispered – her face was pale.

'I know Harriet and him are old friends ... and ...'
She was breathing faster. 'And we know Granddad is
no stranger to secrets, but *this*? I can't ... what ... why
would—'

'FREEZE!' a voice yelled in the doorway. It was the
guard. And, as Phil had earlier noted, he did indeed
have a gun.

Chapter 10

There was an awkward silence in Harriet Goffe's office – just the rain on the glass and the occasional grumble from the electric weather outside. The security guard, wearing a smart, dark blue shirt and a thick black belt – heavy with a baton and a torch – didn't seem to know what to do next. He was pointing a silver pistol at them, with all eight fingers wrapped tight around the grip.

'Don't ... don't move a muscle,' he said, jutting the gun forwards. He stepped inside the room properly. 'W-what are you doing in here?'

'We were wondering if you have a few moments to talk about the Lord Jesus Christ,' Dee said.

'Is that supposed to be funny?' The guard looked

nervous – he didn't seem to be in a joking mood. 'Hands up,' he said, lifting the barrel towards Tim. Without protest, he held his arms above his head.

Tim's heart was going into overdrive while he tried to process just how much trouble they were in and, more so, how much trouble *he* would be in if they were captured. Everything had gone wrong so quickly. He tried to get his thoughts straight, about Eisenstone, about Harriet, but that proved impossible. One thing at a time. All that mattered was that they got out of here with that memory stick.

Despite his manic mind, he did notice that the security guard, although large and scary, had an empty clip on his belt where, Tim surmised, his radio *should* be. This meant backup wasn't on its way.

'You all right there?' Dee asked him.

'Shut it!' He was aiming at her now, shaking. 'How did you get in here?'

'You seem anxious,' she went on. 'Is this your first shift or something?'

'No,' he huffed. 'It's my *second*.'

'Look,' Dee said, 'we are sort of in the wrong – this

is a crime, we get that. *But* how bad would you look if your boss knew that someone broke in on your watch?'

'A couple of children,' Tim added.

'Couple of children and a handsome finger monkey,' Phil said from the desk.

The guard yelped, only now noticing him. Out of impulse he fired a shot – the room flashed bright, the bullet sending splinters and dust spitting from the surface, right next to Phil.

A high-pitched ringing faded in Tim's ears. Phil was staring at the hole by his side, stunned in silence.

'Whoa,' Dee said, slowly pulling her hands away from her head. 'Man, jeez, you've got to relax. You can't shoot guns at children. In virtually no context is that all right.'

'Really,' Tim added. 'It's a no-no.'

Dee shook her head. 'Put it down.'

'What the hell is that thing?!' he demanded, still bemused by Phil. 'And *what* are you doing here?'

'We're here for that,' Tim said, tilting his head at the imagination box on the low coffee table in the corner. He was still wearing the reader. 'Open it up, and this will all make sense.'

Glancing at the contraption, then again, the man seemed to distrust Tim. He took a sidestep towards it. 'What's inside?'

'Have a look.'

He stopped. 'Both of you, face down on the floor.'

Tim nodded to Dee, and they did as he said – Phil was still staring down at what nearly killed him. Smelling the carpet, Tim looked across as the man approached the imagination box. Out of sight, he heard the lid flick open. The guard then stepped back, coughed, and went thudding to the ground.

'Sleep tight,' Tim said, standing, placing his sleeve over his mouth. 'Don't breathe that.'

As Phil was still stuck in a state of shock, Tim picked him up and slipped him into his top pocket. Dee snatched the memory stick, full now with the vital incriminating evidence. Then they made for the door, giving the thick cloud of sleeping gas a wide berth. On the way Tim grabbed the imagination box, dropped it in his rucksack and shouldered into the corridor where there was more space to teleport.

He put his arm around Dee, hearing more security thumping up the stairwell, shouting orders and warnings.

'Ready?' Tim said, holding the orange teleportation sphere.

'Let's go.'

With his eyes closed, he clicked the button. When he looked again, they were in the same place. 'Um.'

'Quickly, Tim,' she said. 'Must leave now.'

Three security guards appeared at the end of the hall, their eyes glistening in the darkness, spotting Tim and Dee standing, like a pair of lost lemons, directly in front of them.

Tim clicked the button again, but nothing happened. It was jammed or malfunctioning or whatever the word is for when your teleporting ball won't work. He shook it. Bashed it on his palm.

'They're just kids, boss,' one of the guards mumbled. 'Where's Jack?'

Through Harriet's open office, they spotted the

man Tim had encouraged to pass out.

'Grab 'em!' another guard shouted.

They turned and ran. At the end of the corridor they arrived at a silver door, which opened into a narrow chamber – a tall ladder ran up the middle, with steel ribs around it near the top. Behind, Dee snapped a key, waiting in the lock, sealing them inside.

'This goes to the roof,' Tim said.

The door handle tilted, then rattled loudly. 'It's locked,' a muffled voice said. There was a pause, then a hard bang. Then another. The hinges buckled, a screw clinked along the floor.

'These guys are loopy,' Dee said.

She began climbing and Tim followed suit. He was no more than three rungs up when the door behind broke from its frame and the guards came pouring in.

'Faster!' His climbing became a scramble as large hands reached out for his feet.

One got a hold, but Tim shook his leg, his shoe coming off in the man's grasp. At the top of the ladder, Dee fell out of the hatch and on to the roof. A harsh wind howled around her, thick columns of rain cascading. The storm was loud – the height of the building put them right in the midst of it.

Tim swung one leg out, but felt a tight biting pain on his other calf, then his thigh. The guard had him pinned against the ladder. He jolted, trying to get free. Dee grabbed and tugged, but the man was too strong. 'I've got him,' he said.

'Run,' Tim yelled. Dee had the memory stick, the evidence – all that mattered was that *she* got away.

Dee turned – the only place she could go was another hatch across the flat expanse. However, before she was even halfway, it swung open and one, two, three guards came out. Skidding, falling to the ground, she rolled over, and made her way back towards Tim, who was getting pulled lower, back inside, back into the hands of TRAD.

In the rain – as heavy as a power shower – Tim gritted his jaw as he put his imagination to good use. He'd wrapped his arm around the horizontal metal, meaning the guard would need to pry him off – this bought him a few moments. He didn't have time, or strength, to reach inside his bag so, instead, in one fluid motion, he disconnected the plastic clips, yanked it from his back with his free hand and hurled it. Spinning, straps twirling, the rucksack went through the round hatch. Tim had one last go at breaking free, twisting and writhing.

On the roof, one of the men was bolting for Dee, running at the pace of someone intent on a savage tackle. A flash of lightning turned raindrops to crystal, making the world seem, for a moment at least, completely still. The bag, housing the imagination box, landed and the lid fell open – a brand-new orange teleportation sphere bounced out and rolled towards Dee. She snatched it from the ground, her shivering, wet fingers still fumbling when the guard arrived. As the delayed drums of thunder quaked overhead, he dived with all his weight, swinging his heavy arms through nothing but thin air and water.

Dee was gone.

With that, Tim's hand was torn from the ladder. He and the large guard both fell back down the chamber, banging and clanging amid the steel safety cage as they went. Luckily, Tim landed on top of the man, who was groaning in pain, badly winded, as the remaining security bundled around them.

Tim realised, as he was dragged inside, that there was no point in running any more, and certainly no point in fighting. They had him.

Chapter 11

The security guard who had grabbed Tim escorted him through the Diamond Building's offices and past the labs, limping and clutching his side. He also fitted him with handcuffs. Actual handcuffs.

'I'm eleven years old,' Tim said, frowning, looking over his shoulder. 'What do you think I am going to do?'

'You're not going to do anything,' the guard replied, placing his hand on Tim's head. He pulled the reader hat off and looked down at it. 'Without this, you're completely harmless.'

They had collected the imagination box from the roof – Tim had only been reunited with it for a matter of minutes. And now he was taken into what he suspected was an interrogation room. There was a brown plastic chair, just like one from school, tucked under an empty wooden table. Opposite that was a far nicer seat, with blue foam lining. And on the right-hand wall was a wide mirror that Tim imagined was see-through from the other side.

'Now,' the guard said. 'Harriet has requested we hold you until she arrives. She wants to speak to you personally.'

Great, Tim thought to himself, just who he wanted to see.

And with that, the man left.

Without his imagination box or his reader, Tim felt helpless. He had no idea if the teleporter sphere he made actually worked – Dee disappeared, sure, but he couldn't be certain she arrived at Fredric's facility. Plus, even if she did, how long would it take to come and rescue him from these people? He kept running over those emails in his mind, wondering what other secrets they might have found. And Professor Eisenstone ... Tim shook his head again.

Phil clambered out of his top pocket sluggishly,

as though he was oblivious to where they were. The monkey hadn't uttered a word since he was almost shot. He sat cross-legged on the table, lost in thought.

'Right,' Tim said. 'Listen, we've got to get out of here – this is bad. We need to escape. Can you pick locks?'

Phil just stared at nothing in particular, without responding.

'Hello? Can you hear me? What's got into you? Look, Harriet is going to be here soon. I have no idea what she's going to do with me. Or you for that matter. Phil, Phil!'

The monkey finally lifted his head, making eye contact. 'I nearly died,' he said.

'Yes. Nearly, but you didn't.'

'That security guard – he shot at me.'

'You made him jump. He didn't mean it. Now, try and get these cuffs off.'

'What is the point?'

'Pardon?' Tim snapped. 'What's the point in getting me out of here? Did you not hear me? Harriet, the woman who, for some unacceptable reason, wants me dead, is coming. I'll level with you, Phil, cards on the table: I don't fully understand what's going on, but I am scared. This place, this situation, it *scares* me.'

'I meant what is the point in anything?'

'Oh, Phil. This isn't the time.'

'My whole life flashed before my tiny eyes when that gun went off. Timothy, do you know what I saw?'

'No?' Tim sighed, tugging at the restraints behind him – the metal was tight on his wrist bones.

'Nothing. My short existence has amounted to nothing. What have I achieved?' Phil stood. 'Hmm? What am I for? I live in a drawer, Timothy.'

'I …'

'A drawer.'

'This … these are very grand questions, Phil, and they apply to us all.'

'You were right, good sir, it most certainly is not all sunshine and sing-alongs.'

'We can discuss this later, just help me get my cuffs off.'

There was a crackling sound and Tim spotted a speaker in the corner of the room, near the ceiling.

A voice boomed from within. 'Tim, we can see *and* hear you. This is a two-way mirror.'

'I did suspect it was,' Tim said under his breath. 'Never mind, Phil. You probably won't have to worry about the meaning of life for much longer.'

Half an hour passed in near silence. Tim and Phil stared into space, both pondering their respective crises. Eventually, Tim gulped at the sound of a female voice behind the door – a darkened shape through the frosted window. A few seconds later, Harriet entered. The gentle breeze of her moving through the room was enough to make Tim's neck hair tingle.

Knowing what he knew, he saw her differently. Before, she seemed like a stern head teacher, a neutral authority figure, but now she was more of a menacing presence – her narrow, wandering eyes were almost reptilian.

'Tim,' she said, as she pulled her blue chair out to sit. 'Have they been treating you well, have— Are those handcuffs?!'

Harriet stood, left the room and returned with some keys to free Tim from the restraints. He rubbed his wrists as the metal clanked on to the table next to Phil, who was still slouching. 'I am sorry about that,' she said. 'The guards seem scared of you for some reason – they think your imagination box is dangerous. You'll be pleased to hear that Jack has woken up from his short slumber.'

She was being far too nice, Tim thought. This might have fooled him before, but not now.

'You could be in a huge amount of trouble,' Harriet said, pulling her long, blonde, tightly plaited hair round in front of her shoulder – it hung down, almost to her waist. 'But I must admit, I am more curious than angry. Can I ask what on earth you and your friend were up to? Did you eat Chinese food in my office?'

Tim frowned, then remembered the fortune cookie. He decided to pretend he hadn't read those emails – best she didn't know that he knew. 'We were looking for my imagination box,' he said.

'You found it in a cupboard I understand?'

'That's right. I imagined a tracking device would appear inside it, then I knew it was here. Dee did the rest.'

'Hmm,' she said, tapping her chin. 'I wonder ... I wonder who hid it there, and why?'

'Yes,' Tim added, with slight sarcasm. 'It is a mystery.'

'So you found it, but that doesn't explain why you were in *my* office?'

Discovering that you're an unhinged nutbag, Tim thought.

She sighed. 'It's fine, it doesn't even matter. Because something else has come up. Listen, I need you to do something for me. Remember I told you about the Mind Surfer?'

Here we go, Tim thought. She was going to try to distract him, divert his attention elsewhere. He hoped once again that Dee had got that memory stick out of here. If it got to Fredric it would only be a matter of time before someone arrived and blew this whole thing wide open, exposed Harriet for who she really was. A sad thought followed this ... again, he just couldn't comprehend what he'd read about Eisenstone.

'Some of the more elaborate conspiracy theories about the elusive individual suggest he or she is controlling people on a *huge* scale. Nationally. Even internationally.'

'Right?' Tim said, curious, but still convinced this was just some yarn, another one of Harriet's elaborate lies.

'Anyway, Fredric … he …' She sat forwards, throwing her long snake of blonde hair over her shoulder, out of sight. 'You've seen his facility – that's where you've been, right – in Nevada? I need you—'

The door swung open with a bang. A guard and a man wearing a dark suit with a black tie entered. Harriet turned in her chair to look at them. 'Can I help you, gentlemen?'

'You're under arrest, Mrs Goffe,' the suited man said. 'You do not have to say anything, but it may harm your defence if you do not mention when questioned something which you later rely on in court.'

The guard snatched up the cuffs Tim had just been wearing, and firmly clicked them on to the wrists of his own boss. The teleportation sphere *had* worked – Dee clearly got the memory stick to Fredric who had, in turn, alerted these agents.

'There must be some kind of mistake,' Harriet said, her eyes rolling and darting in what looked like genuine confusion.

Tim smiled, awash with relief – seeing right through her crocodile tears – as they escorted TRAD's director from the interrogation room.

Chapter 12

Tim looked up through the metal struts of the huge roller coaster he'd just created in front of his castle – his pretend sun casting its curled shadow across him. Beyond the twisting, undulating track he saw the roof high above – right in the centre was the circular service hatch. For the briefest moment he felt an odd sense of sadness that the imagination space, despite its infinite variables, would always have a ceiling. He would never, unless of course he imagined them, be able to look at the stars from this place.

Things had changed quickly at the Technology, Research and Defence agency following Harriet's arrest. The emails Tim and Dee discovered on her computer were just the tip of the iceberg. In fact, there were hundreds of incriminating documents on her hard drive – enough to send her down for a long time. They pinned the murder of the lollipop lady on her, as well as a long list of charges Tim hadn't even heard of. Despite all of this, she denied everything.

TRAD itself was disbanded – people were on the news, clearing their desks, as the Diamond Building was shut down. What struck Tim was how fast it all happened. By the end of that week, in fact, the organisation was no longer operating. Even the Prime Minister took to television to explain that a previously secret department had 'failed' in its job to protect the public from dangerous forces.

The news said that Daniel Moore – a former TRAD agent, who had exchanged those emails with Harriet – was the Mind Surfer. He too found himself behind bars.

And, most incredibly of all, Professor Eisenstone was arrested. He protested his innocence – denying all knowledge of having been offered payment by Harriet. Both Tim and Dee had wanted to speak with him – to hear his side of the story – but they hadn't been allowed to. However, a few days later, the professor had phoned Tim directly to tell him that he had done nothing wrong.

'I, I must be quick. They think I'm speaking to my lawyer,' Eisenstone had said. 'I don't know why but, indeed, someone wants me in prison.'

The image of Eisenstone locked away did seem wrong. The professor was many things, but surely not a criminal?

'But, then, what about the emails?' Tim asked.

'It's a frame-up. Listen, I don't know how far …' There had been a noise in the background, someone telling Eisenstone to hurry up. 'Please, Tim, you have to believe me. You have to find the truth.'

The phone then went dead. Tim hadn't been able to contact him after that.

While all this was happening, Tim, Dee and Phil travelled between home and the imagination space as Fredric wanted to do more experiments. At first they had to walk across town to a Wilde Tech office in Glassbridge, not far from school, where they teleported to Fredric's London building and then, once again, to Nevada.

However, after a few goes, Tim created a teleportation sphere – which he kept in his bedroom. This, in effect, meant that his wardrobe opened directly to the top floor of his bespoke castle – endless wonders behind a thin wooden door.

Despite this, however, Tim felt so lost and unsure that he just couldn't enjoy his creations.

'Do you think we've made a mistake?' Tim said to Dee, who was taking pictures of the latest addition to the space on her phone.

Another thing that had shocked him was her total acceptance of her grandfather's imprisonment. When they read those emails, Dee looked as shocked as Tim. But, over the past few days, she appeared to have come to terms with it all. Even by her standards, she seemed notably cold.

'No way, this roller coaster was the best idea you've had,' Dee said, clicking away.

'I mean with what happened at TRAD?'

'This again? We've won,' Dee said, pocketing her

mobile. 'Box is back, Harriet's been arrested, Daniel too. Case closed. Victory dance.'

'What about Eisenstone? In your heart, do you *honestly* believe he would do something like this? Work with people like that?'

'In my heart? Maybe not. But in my head? You saw those emails, that *evidence*.' She shrugged. 'I guess there will be a trial – we'll know *why* he did what he did then.'

'Look, I know you don't "do" emotions, but come on.'

'What do you mean?'

'You don't seem at all bothered,' Tim said.

'Yeah, it sucks, but Granddad has always been full of secrets – you know that.'

'But why would they do all this?'

'You said yourself, Granddad didn't like you having the imagination box – especially not when you break promises and take it out of your room. And TRAD knew it was dangerous – they knew all about Crowfield House. Maybe they just wanted the technology off the streets? As I said, we'll know all the ins and outs soon enough ... Anyway, we gonna ride this thing?' Dee looked up at the roller coaster's bright, stripy blue and orange cart.

Earlier that day Tim had created another fortune cookie, just like the one with Harriet's password. He imagined the contents would say whether or not Eisenstone was really guilty. When he cracked it open, the piece of paper simply read 'No'.

Initially Tim thought that was definitive proof, but Dee explained, logically, that it was probably just what he wanted to believe.

'Remember when I was doing my schoolwork in the imagination box?' Tim said. 'I had this weird feeling the whole time. I felt as though I hadn't earned it. As though I'd cut corners. As though I hadn't ... I dunno ... I hadn't done the job properly. That's how I feel now.'

'Oh,' Phil moaned from Tim's top pocket. 'It's so simple for you two. You have all these outlandish adventures and this fandangled technology to play with. But what about me? What is my purpose? Timothy, you cannot create sentient beings and relinquish all responsibility – these are not rhetorical questions.'

The monkey's identity crisis had gone from bad to worse since his near-death experience. Even when Tim created him a hovering 'motor-bicycle', he barely rode it.

Last year Eisenstone had told Tim that he really shouldn't make any more 'living' things in his imagination box. Apparently it was 'unethical' and 'risky'. Maybe it was exactly this kind of thing that he was wary of?

'Perhaps you should do something creative,' Tim suggested. 'Rechannel these insecurities.'

They clambered up the narrow stairs – their feet clanging – and into the roller coaster's metal cart. The cushioned, leather-covered safety pads came down over his shoulders.

Right then Tim decided, for certain, that *his* heart was right. That fortune cookie was right. Eisenstone wouldn't lie. Somewhere along the line they'd made a terrible error. Now, Tim had another tricky task ahead of him. Somehow, he had to prove the professor's innocence.

The cart ticked up the track – *clunk, clunk, clunk* – higher and higher.

Still ascending, overlooking everything he'd created, Tim thought of the news they'd watched and of Samantha Locke's unmistakable red hair. He recalled her vanilla perfume, remembered the jazzy music they'd whispered beneath in his room that day.

There will come a time when you run out of answers, she had told him. The cart reached the highest point, tilted and, with a held breath, Tim waited for it to fall.

The following day, Tim, Dee and Phil paid Samantha Locke a visit. Still filled with doubt about what had happened, Tim was keen to speak with her – whereas Dee was, for some reason, quite reluctant.

However, she came round to the idea and they hopped aboard a train. Elisa was still apathetic about Tim's comings and goings and gave her permission without much thought. In fact, she didn't even ask where they were going. Tim, as always, assumed she was simply busy, although it was decidedly strange how little she seemed to care.

The journalist lived on the second floor of a gloomy block of flats. In the alleyway that led to the door Tim looked up through the metal frames of the fire escapes – there was a thin strip of overcast charcoal sky above, between the close buildings.

Inside, Samantha clicked, clunked and slid closed a series of locks.

'Sorry about the mess,' she said.

Tim paused in the doorway of the living room, taking in the walls of newspaper cuttings, notes, photos and hundreds of documents. There was no furniture besides a single desk, also covered in this stuff.

'It's, well ...' Samantha added, running her hand through her short rusty hair. 'It's not exactly the Ritz.' She seemed embarrassed. 'I have beanbags we can sit on.'

While she fetched them, Tim and Dee whispered to one another. 'I think we should leave,' she said.

'What? Why?'

'This woman is clearly crazy. I bet she collects cats.'

'No.'

'Probable bad egg. Dodgy. Getting vibes.'

'Inclined to concur,' Phil added. 'Monkey Sellotaper.'

'Let's just hear what she has to say. Besides, she's on TV – they don't let bad people on TV.'

'Do either of you want a drink?' Samantha asked, returning and dropping three small fabric beanbags on the floor. 'I've got . . . water? Or . . . maybe you could create something for us, in your . . . imagination box?'

Tim frowned, defensively lifting his rucksack up on his shoulder.

'I've told you, I read TRAD's files on you, front to back – I know everything.'

This was actually refreshing – to be able to be completely honest. Tim shrugged and got his imagination box out and the three of them sat round it, as though it was a campfire. He created a small pot of tea and some (perhaps unduly civilised) cups and saucers, complete with little rings of gold around the rims. Phil too enjoyed a miniature version of everything they had – his little finger jutted out as he sipped.

After Samantha had asked about the box and about Phil, as people tended to, she asked how she could help them.

'It's about . . . the Mind Surfer,' Tim said.

'What do you want to know? Apparently they've caught him.'

'You told me to come and see you when I ran out of answers. I just can't believe Professor Eisenstone would lie, would break the law. It doesn't add up.'

'Ah,' Samantha said. 'Welcome to my world. Not adding up is the Mind Surfer's thing. As you can see, I've been trying to crack this one for a long while.'

She pointed their attention to the wall of newspaper cuttings and documents. There was one picture that seemed to take centre stage in all the evidence – it was of her and a man, standing in glossy, brightly coloured jumpsuits. Behind them, in the background, was a small aeroplane covered in sunlight.

'Joseph,' Samantha said, in a low tone. 'That's us in Australia. We'd been skydiving together. He was my . . . my husband.' She blew out some air, composed herself and then nodded.

'What exactly happened to him?' Tim asked.

'He was a reporter too. He worked for a couple of large newspapers in London – mostly freelance. It all started after the riots, which I'm sure you saw on TV?'

Tim remembered the news – he *had* seen footage of riots, but thought nothing of it at the time.

'He interviewed some people involved,' Samantha went on. 'What he found was very strange – you see, the riots in towns all across the UK, they started at exactly the same time.'

'Could it not simply be that people heard about them, social media and that,' Dee suggested, 'then decided they might be able to loot a few shops? Free trainers are enticing.'

'Yes,' Samantha said. 'That was exactly what everyone believed. But, if you look at the CCTV footage, the incidents began at *precisely* the same time. As in, to the second.'

'Do the police know this?' Tim asked.

'Well, yes, but they haven't given it any weight.

They said that protests started the whole thing.'

'That sounds more likely.' Dee placed her mug down, then checked the time on her phone, glancing at Tim. This was a hint to leave, but he ignored her.

'You know, that's what I said,' Samantha added. 'I told Joseph he was crazy. But then there were the carrots. Did you see *that* on the news?'

'Yes,' Dee said. 'I understand that was an internet thing – viral stunt or whatever.'

'Again, that's what people *thought*. Everyone agreeing to buy carrots on the same day? Ha ha, very funny. But there was no campaign, no group. The sharp rise in carrot sales occurred at precisely the same time – 2 p.m. It wasn't until the following day that the media even took notice. It was as though everyone, at exactly the same moment, decided to buy carrots. When asked, the shoppers couldn't explain their behaviour. Joseph thought, like the riots, it was the work of the Mind Surfer. That he was testing how people could be controlled.'

Dee coughed, slyly glaring – eyes wide with

concern – at Tim. Samantha seemed to notice.

'You think I'm insane,' she said. 'That's fine. When Joseph showed me everything he'd found, I thought that too.'

'How did he die?' Tim asked.

'He wrote up the story, but, before he could file it ... one quiet Sunday afternoon he wandered from our house to a nearby building site, clambered through a fence and then climbed up to the top of a crane. He walked calmly to the end. Without hesitation, he stepped off and fell to his death.'

'That's terrible,' Tim said.

'He was under strain from work. But I don't think it would have led him to do that. He wasn't himself. It was as though he was ... possessed.'

Tim had read similar stories of 'possession'. Over the past week he and Dee had googled 'the Mind Surfer' countless times, only to read countless posts on countless forums written by people Dee sensitively described as 'absolute whack-job loons'. She had a point – conspiracy theorists do tend to be a certain type of person.

Samantha stood and walked to the wall of

evidence. 'I think the Mind Surfer *was* experimenting with the technology and knew that in order to keep it under wraps he had to kill Joseph. Who knows how many other people have had to die to keep this secret.'

Tim then spoke about the lollipop lady who had stolen his box, and the first man who had jumped into the water chasing him, but then seemed to 'snap out of it'.

'Perhaps the shock of the cold brought him to his senses,' Samantha said. 'That's interesting...'

'Having struggled with the many perils of being self-aware,' Phil added, 'perhaps being controlled might not be such a bad thing.'

'Ignore him,' Tim said. 'He's having a crisis.'

Samantha smiled. 'But, hey,' she said, shrugging. 'At least I won't have to spend any more time in jail at the hands of TRAD – they certainly didn't like me snooping around. I guess now we know why ... Anyway, it's over, right? Daniel Moore, a rogue TRAD agent ... done and dusted. Thanks to you guys the Mind Surfer is behind bars.'

Tim felt just as unsettled when they left – none of

what Samantha told them went any way to explaining how or why Professor Eisenstone had ended up involved in all this. That part still didn't fit.

They headed to the station to get the train back to Glassbridge. Tim suggested a sneaky teleport to save time but, as it made Dee queasy, they decided to take the old-fashioned route.

They waited on the platform, sitting on the cold metal bench. There wasn't a single soul in sight – just the straight track disappearing off to the left and to the right. Dee was, as usual, engrossed in her phone. Tim, however, was still wondering *how* someone would be able to take over members of the public.

'When the Mind Surfer took control, how come the signal didn't affect everyone?' Tim said.

Dee didn't respond.

'Quite an acute observation, Timothy,' Phil said, looking up from his pocket.

'It couldn't be a blanket transmission,' Tim added. 'It'd need to be directed at individuals. But how would that work?'

'Hmm, yeah, whatever,' Dee said. 'Or, like, the

carrots and riots were nothing to do with it and Samantha's madness is contagious?'

'Your mum's right,' Tim said. 'You do spend too much time on your mobile.'

'What else is there to look at between doing things?' she said. 'Besides, she's started making absurd rules to restrict it. She's explicitly banned me from using it in the bath, for example.'

'You use your phone in the bath?' Tim said.

'Well, not any more – I nearly dropped it in the other day. Was a close call. These things ain't waterproof.'

Tim's heartbeat steadily sped up. 'What did you say?'

'Three stars!' Dee said, proudly turning her IcoRama towards him, showing her 90,000 score on Squirrel Boarder.

And there was the answer, hiding in plain sight.

'It'd need to be an electronic device capable of sending and receiving signals, that people had close to them at all times ... my God.' Tim grabbed her arm. 'Dee. It's phones. The Mind Surfer was controlling people through mobiles. It makes sense. That's why the man who chased me stopped when he jumped into the river. *The water* – it broke his phone. He couldn't be controlled any more.'

Dee's head dipped. She set her IcoRama face down on the bench by her thigh. 'That's not true, Tim,' she said. 'Do not say it again.'

'We've got to tell Samantha, Fredric, everyone. If the technology is still in place, what's there to stop someone else doing it? We would need proof, we'd need something substantial …' Tim turned to her. 'Dee?'

Her face was blank. She simply stared back with empty eyes.

'Dee …?'

She struck like a coiled snake, wrapping her hands around Tim's neck, squeezing with an incredible amount of force. At first he thought she was joking. 'Wha—' Tim wheezed, trying to push her off. 'This … isn't … funny.'

Teeth exposed, she shoved him down on to the ground and began to strangle him. Phil bounced out of his pocket and rolled under the bench. Turning red, purple, Tim flailed his arms, clawing at her face. He punched and grabbed Dee's wrists, but she was too strong, her grip too tight.

Tim croaked. 'Th – the – the ph – ph …' he managed, his vision narrowing, a throb growing in his head as Dee pressed the life from him. 'Sm – smash her phone.'

The monkey turned, leapt up on to the bench, grabbed Dee's mobile, lifted it and jumped off, pile-driving it into the paving. The screen cracked, but it was still alight.

Tim thrust his weight up, trying to buck Dee off, but it was no use. Her thumbs dug in, his face ached with the heat of blood. As he began to feel numb, out of the corner of his eye, he saw Phil swing the silver IcoRama above his head and slam it on the ground with all his might. Bang, bang, bang, until—

There was a loud gasp of air from Tim's lungs as Dee fell off, grabbing her hair and trying to understand what was going on.

'What … what's happening?' She slid to a sitting

position on the station platform. 'Oh my God,' she yelled, looking at Phil. 'You broke my phone.'

'So there we go,' Tim said, with a cough. 'We have got it wrong … the Mind Surfer is still very much at large.'

Chapter 13

Tim and Dee were sitting, facing one another, on the cold concrete of the train station platform. Between them, Phil stood amid the innards of her IcoRama phone – glass, green circuitry, chips. It looked like the tiny monkey had murdered a tiny robot.

'What's going on?' Dee asked again, scrambling to a kneeling position. She rubbed her temple. 'Why has Phil broken my phone?'

'You became crazed,' the monkey replied. 'You tried to strangle poor Timothy.'

'For real?'

'Seemed pretty real to me,' Tim gasped, holding his throat and clambering back on to the bench. He brushed the gravel from his jeans and straightened his hat. 'The Mind Surfer is out there.'

'And Timothy's theory of mobile phones being intrinsically linked to his operation is accurate,' Phil added.

'So … wait, they were taking me over to use me to kill you?'

'Yes, because I figured it out, because I'm a genius. It's all coming together,' Tim said, looking up at the winter sky. 'That's how you knew where the imagination box was. You said you just had a *feeling* it was in that cupboard. Someone was guiding you. Maybe that's why you were so keen not to investigate now. Why you thought Samantha was crazy. Why you accepted so quickly that your granddad was involved.'

Dee was shaking her head. She seemed overwhelmed by the news, by the idea that her thoughts had not been her own. What else had the Mind Surfer changed about her personality? What else had she done against her will?

'That means whoever stole the imagination box

planted it there for us to find,' Tim added. 'Samantha was right. It is all connected to me.'

'But why?'

'I too am curious about the specifics of this plot,' Phil added. 'Especially as you own an IcoRama phone as well, Timothy.'

'Yes,' Tim said, grabbing it from his pocket. 'You're right.'

'So why aren't *you* under the Mind Surfer's command?' Dee asked.

'Maybe you are,' Phil added, bulging his eyes and wiggling his fingers. 'Oooo.'

Tim dropped his phone on to the ground, next to Dee's, and repeatedly stamped on it – the frame buckling, plastic casing and small screws bouncing – until it was just bits.

'It's probably because you created it yourself I reckon,' Dee concluded, glancing between him and the debris. 'It's not really a proper one, is it?'

'Oh yeah,' Tim said, standing up straight, realising he hadn't needed to smash it. 'Better safe than sorry.' He shrugged.

'If there is truth to these suspicions, as I suspect there is, I feel we must tell Fredric,' Phil added. 'And Samantha. She will be most elated to hear, I am sure.'

'Good idea.' Tim nodded. 'Let's call them.'

'How?' Dee asked, picking up a wire with a miniature microphone dangling.

'Pay phone?'

'Are pay phones not fictional?' Phil wondered. 'I thought they were like telegrams. Or carrier pigeons. Or sea horses.'

'All of those things are real,' Tim said.

'Even sea horses?' The monkey's face lit up.

'Even sea horses.'

Tim grabbed his rucksack and they headed down the quiet street in front of the train station. After a short walk they found a phone box, proving to Phil that they weren't mythical.

'How quaint,' he said, leaping from Tim's pocket on to the top of the handset, before clambering up higher, standing in front of a wall of scruffy flyers. 'I fear, in this day and age, this contraption lacks a purpose.' He frowned, looking at his feet. 'A little like me,' he whispered.

'Phil, you're meant to be a secret monkey. Back inside.' Tim held his shirt out and, after a short pout with flopped arms, the monkey scurried back into his hiding place. Tim rummaged, patting himself down. 'Has anyone got 20p?'

'Make one,' Dee sighed. 'Sometimes I think you forget about having *an imagination box*.'

'That's an actual crime – counterfeiting money.'

'Again, how many times, why does it matter if you're not going to get caught?'

Tim rolled his eyes and half agreed. Dee was often somehow right and wrong all at the same time. He threw his bag off his back then imagined, as clearly as always, a coin for the telephone. The device trembled quietly for a moment, then he slid the lid open. It shone – clean and new – from the bottom of the metal box. Instead of the Queen's face, the head side of the coin featured Dee.

'There,' he said. 'This'll confuse someone one day.'

The coin clinked home and Tim lifted the handset,

reading from the card Samantha had given him. The moment she answered, he double-checked what kind of phone she had; she told him hers was more than ten years old, with a dated green screen.

'Good,' Tim said. 'Now, can you remember what kind your husband had?'

'What?' Samantha seemed confused.

'His mobile. What brand was it?'

'I . . . he . . . he'd just got a new one,' Samantha said, stuttering to remember. 'That's right, he showed me how good the camera was. It was an IcoRama 2020.'

Bingo.

'Samantha, I think I know how the Mind Surfer is controlling people.'

Tim explained, Phil and Dee crammed behind him in the tight space, shouting out supporting comments. The final piece of the puzzle, which confirmed it all, fell into place. Samantha's husband *was* murdered by the Mind Surfer. And, if it wasn't for Phil, the truth would have died again right there on the station platform.

'My God,' Samantha said after an astonished pause.

Tim heard her scoop keys off a table. 'Wait there. I'm coming to get you. Have you told anyone else?'

'No. I called you first. I'll phone Fredric now.'

'Don't,' Samantha said quickly. 'Stay off all phones. This needs to be reported face to face. Who knows who's listening.'

No more than ten minutes later, her car skidded to a stop in front of them. 'Get in.'

Tim and Dee leapt into the back seat, the imagination box between them in the middle. Samantha passed through a thick folder. 'That's some background on IcoRama,' she said. 'They're a giant company and are clearly affiliated, in some capacity, with the Mind Surfer. We need to get as much dirt as we can before we expose them. Fredric – he can help?'

'Yes,' Tim said.

They headed towards Wilde Tech's offices.

Samantha instructed Tim and Dee to look through the documents as she drove – they were searching for any information that could link the business to anything that had happened to Tim. He wondered again why he had been targeted. What they had to gain from stealing his imagination box, from entwining him in all of TRAD's politics. And again, he felt a surge of energy towards finding the truth – to prove Eisenstone's innocence.

The car came off a slip road and pulled on to the motorway – it was getting late now, the dusk light casting shadows on shadows. The indicator clunked – Tim watched Samantha check her mirror, then blind spot, then cut across the white lines and into the fast lane. They must have been exceeding ninety miles per hour – Tim saw the world zip past, his eyes juddering to keep up.

'If IcoRama are behind this,' Samantha was saying as she drove, 'then we'll need to go public with what we find. If they're able to silence anyone, the only way they can be beaten is exposure. Everyone has to know the truth. And all at the same time.'

'What do you know about them?' Tim asked.

'Not much – only that the company was in trouble last year,' Samantha said. 'Falling profits, big losses. Then some other business took over ... they sacked the board of directors … was all a bit controversial. Someone wanted to take control of IcoRama and wanted to do it quickly. Now we just need to find out who.'

By his side, Dee was licking her thumb, flicking through the sheets of paper.

'How you doing, Dee?' Samantha asked. 'Can you remember what it felt like when you weren't yourself?'

'Yes and no,' she said. 'I can kind of remember little bits, but there are blanks too – it was just that I had no control. When we broke into the Diamond Building, I just had a feeling – an urge – to look in that cupboard. And when I strangled Tim, it was just like a reflex. Like blinking – kind of automatic. I'm a bit miffed about my phone though. Loved that thing.'

'Even though it was taking control of your brain?' Tim asked.

'That was certainly a down side,' she admitted.

'Is that why you've been so materialistic too?' Tim wondered. 'You were being controlled?'

'Nah, a lot of that's just me.'

'It's insane,' Samantha added, thinking aloud.

'IcoRama's profits over the last few months have been monumental. Those phones are all over the *world*. We've got to stop them.'

Tim looked out of the window as they overtook a large green jeep. The driver – an old man with a blue body warmer and mutton-chop sideburns – had a hands-free set in his ear.

'So ... you strangled me when I'd figured out that it was the phones ...' Tim said, still piecing it all together. 'That means the Mind Surfer was controlling you *right then*. He ... they were watching through your eyes, listening through your ears. So ... they know.'

'What do you mean?' Samantha said.

'They know that we know.'

'So anyone with an IcoRama phone ...' Dee said, slowly, catching up. Tim could only see Samantha's eyes in the rear-view mirror – she looked concerned. Her foot pushed on to the accelerator, picking up further speed. '... is a danger.'

Then, on cue, the jeep by their side smashed into the car. Samantha yelled, grasping at the steering wheel as they swerved and bounced off the motorway barrier – dust and sparks shrieking. They returned to the tarmac – Tim grabbed the back of the seat, turning and watching the four-wheel drive drift away, across two lanes now, getting ready for a second go.

'Hold on!' Samantha screamed as they collided again – glass from the front and back windows exploding inside, the roar of the motorway tearing into the car. Sheets of paper were swirling, madly slapping around them.

In what seemed like slow motion, Tim watched the jeep prepare for a third and, by the look of it, final ram. The driver's face was blank, like the man who had chased Tim through the market, like the lollipop lady, like Dee when she strangled him. Time sped back up as he yanked his steering wheel, hurtling towards them, but – moments before impact – Samantha stamped on the brakes.

As steam screeched around them, the jeep whipped in front, missing the car and slamming into the metal barrier, tilting and rolling over and over, once vertically, in a haze of mud and spiralling shrapnel. A piece of wheel arch grazed the windscreen as Samantha rammed the gear stick forwards and continued on.

Tim looked behind – silently hoping the driver was OK – but without a beat, a sports car barrelled towards them. Next to it was a van and beyond that was a large lorry – all the drivers' faces were empty.

'They're going to kill us,' Samantha said, weaving between vehicles, changing lanes.

'Do something, Tim,' Dee said, pushing his rucksack towards him. The sports car connected with the rear bumper, jolting everyone. Dee grabbed the armrest, her other hand on the ceiling. 'Sort of nowish.'

Trying his best to ignore the chaos and noise, Tim buried his face in his hands, imagining something to drag the odds into their favour. He unzipped his bag and pulled the box out. Opening the lid, he held it up by the broken window as one, two, three and then *hundreds* of metal spikes poured out. The road behind was littered with a trail of them. Their pursuers weaved and dodged but, one by one, tyres exploded and they skidded, some swerving off, others spinning complete circles, as though on ice, bashing into one another.

'Ha ha!' Tim yelled. 'Spikes solve everything.'

'Superb work, Timothy,' Phil agreed.

'Got any ideas for that?' Samantha asked.

Up ahead, Tim saw what appeared to be a roadblock – ten or more vehicles all parked at unusual angles, across every lane.

'This is turning into quite a high-profile incident,' Dee said. 'They sure are desperate to get us.'

'Just shows how right we must be,' Samantha said.

Instead of stopping, Tim noticed she put her foot down – the revs picked up, the worry mounted.

'What . . . what exactly are you planning here?' Tim asked, concerned.

The car then slowed down dramatically. 'I was going to ram through, like in a film,' she said. 'But then I realised we'd probably all die.'

'Yes,' Dee said. 'It'd just be a car crash, wouldn't it?'

'Off-road it is then.'

They left the motorway and rumbled down a bank – branches whipped the bonnet, leaves flurried inside. Towards the bottom of the slope the vehicle's left wheels rode up on to a tree stump – Tim yelled out as the car went rolling over, crashing, smashing and bouncing on to its roof.

Upside down, suspended by seat belts, everybody groaned – the stench of exhaust fumes and damp earth swept into Tim's nose as the engine sputtered out. For the second time that day, his head throbbed and his cheeks flashed hot.

With his trademark agility, Phil scurried on to the ceiling – now the floor – and looked up. 'I must confess, that was my first time on this motorway,' the monkey said. 'Is it usually like that?'

'Generally there are fewer crashes,' Dee said in a pained voice. 'But otherwise, yes.'

They unclipped themselves, all taking care not to get cut on the glass crunching below them. Tim and Dee clambered out first, then helped Samantha crawl through the open window.

At the top of the bank a police car had pulled up,

its fluorescent stripes on white paint unmistakable through the foliage.

'Oh thank *God*,' Dee said, brushing herself off, as two large officers trudged down towards them. 'Have we got a story for you.'

But, as they arrived, Tim noticed that familiar glaze in their eyes. 'Wait,' he said, 'they're not . . .'

As Samantha realised and turned, one of the policeman grabbed her shoulder, tugging her back. Phil leapt from Tim, scuttled across a branch and jumped on to his hand. The officer barely reacted as the monkey bit down. With a straight face he just held his arm out and the other man grabbed Phil and squeezed him within his leather glove.

'Release me from this fingery prison,' Phil yelled.

'Get the kids,' one of the officers said in a neutral voice, staring between Tim and Dee. He then dragged Samantha and Phil away, up the hill.

Before they succumbed to a similar fate, Dee pulled Tim's arm and they took off running across the nearby field. Now it was just the two of them . . . against, it seemed, the rest of the world.

Chapter 14

They arrived somewhere dark and cramped. Tim felt his shoulder awkwardly bent across his face, and could smell Dee's slightly coconutty shampoo.

'What the . . .?' she said, her voice loud in Tim's ear. 'Where are we?'

Reaching out he found a latch and pulled it down. They tumbled out into his bedroom. Back at the Dawn Star.

'Why are we here?' he said, holding on to the orange ball he kept in his cupboard.

The dead-eyed men in high-visibility jackets had locked Samantha and Phil in their car, next to the gridlocked motorway.

Tim and Dee, however, had ducked through a fence and run, as fast as their legs would carry them, across a field. The jagged rocks and rolled earth made for rough going. Stumbling, panting, Tim had looked back to the road to see they weren't being followed – he saw Samantha's upturned car, with steam billowing out of the engine. They'd clambered over a broken, rusty, barbed-wire fence and into a wooded area. It was late enough to be near pitch-black under the canopy of trees. Dried brambles tugged at their trousers and their shoes squelched through mud, but they didn't care.

Once out of sight, they crouched. 'I think we're alone now,' Dee had whispered, out of breath. 'There doesn't seem to be anyone around.'

'They took Phil,' Tim said, feeling shock, outrage and wild confusion all at once. 'Controlling members of the public, framing friendly professors, murdering God knows how many people … I could let that go. But stealing my monkey? The Mind Surfer, whoever he is, has just made an enemy.'

'I think you should whip up a mobile,' Dee said.

'Now is *not* the time for Squirrel Boarder.'

'No, let's call Fredric – he said he doesn't use a mobile phone, so he won't be under anyone's command. Let's tell him. At least then, if we die, someone else will know the truth.'

'Why are you saying that? Don't talk about dying.'

'We *could* die,' Dee said. 'In fact, it seems fairly likely.'

'Shush. No.'

Tim again pictured Eisenstone sitting alone in a cell, wrongly imprisoned and miles from home. What other mistakes had they made? Tim wished he could call the professor, wished he could apologise, and promise him once more that he would sort everything out. A reassuring voice could be just what he needed.

But Dee was right – Tim knew that the only person left who could help them was Fredric.

'Shouldn't have taken your imagination box to school, hey,' Dee said.

'That is not a constructive comment.'

Wondering where on earth Phil and Samantha might end up, he did as she said. He found it hard to focus but, after a few false starts, conjured a very primitive mobile in his imagination box. It had an old green screen and the number for Fredric's office landline saved on speed dial. There was no answer, so he flicked through until he found the number for his Nevada facility.

This time he answered on the first ring.

'Listen, Fredric, it's Tim. This is complicated, but some serious stuff is going down.'

'Proper serious,' Dee added. 'The world has gone insane.'

'We got it all wrong, somehow, about Eisenstone, about *everything*,' Tim said. 'The Mind Surfer is still out there.'

'Huh?' Fredric said.

'What do you know about IcoRama phones?' Tim asked.

'Um ... I can't say I know anything about them. Why?'

'They've kidnapped Phil ... and Samantha Locke. She was with us – they've got her too.'

'Hang on, man, dude, slow down.'

'It's ... the Mind Surfer – he's using IcoRama

phones to control people.'

'He's *what*?' Fredric sounded, rightly, incredulous. 'But they caught him. Daniel … he's in prison. We stopped him.'

'No, that's not right.'

Tim explained what had happened and, steadily, Fredric seemed to take it all seriously.

'Right, listen, don't speak to another soul about this. No one can be trusted. Just come here,' Fredric said.

'All right.'

'Have you got a teleportation sphere on you? You can recalibrate it to come straight to my office. I'll meet you there.'

'No,' Tim said. 'But I've got an imagination box.'

'Even better, man, get going.'

As Tim created a blue teleportation sphere, Dee said, 'Someone who works for IcoRama – they can target literally millions of people.'

'Yeah, but we'll go and ruin their mad little party, rescue Phil and Samantha, and clear your granddad's name,' Tim said. 'Bang. Done.'

He pulled the small ball from his imagination box,

swung his rucksack on to his back and put his arm round Dee. He had one last glance across the wide field, the motorway stretching off to their left, over hills and into the distance.

Together they held it, nodding silently, both clicking the button at the same time. Zip-pop, and they were gone – a small amount of water flooded into four empty footprints.

And yet, instead of arriving at Fredric's office, they had appeared here, in Tim's closet.

Again, he tried to create a teleportation sphere that would take them to Fredric but, again, it only managed to transport them to the other side of his bedroom.

'Why won't it work? My imagination performs *so well* when I make random tat for you, but when we *really* need it, it lets us down,' Tim said. 'Stupid box.'

'Relax. At least we're safe – no one knows we're here.'

'I suppose.'

Tim then used the landline on his bedside cabinet

to call Fredric, but there was no answer. He left a message explaining the faulty teleportation spheres.

'Right,' Tim said, dropping the phone. 'The Wilde Tech office in Glassbridge – there's a teleportation sphere there that can take us to London, then straight to the imagination space. We can figure all this out with Fredric. We'll run there, quick style. Straight across town. As long as no one sees—'

The door handle tilted. 'Tim?' Elisa said. But, before she got a foot inside, Dee dived across the carpet and shouldered it shut, and then turned the lock.

Elisa stumbled back in the hall – they heard shocked cursing.

'Wow,' Tim said. 'What are you doing?'

'What kind of phone does Elisa have?' Dee whispered, her back pressed against the wood.

Tim winced, then closed his eyes. 'An IcoRama 2020,' he said. 'Everyone has them . . .'

'What if she's . . .' Dee bobbed her head from side to side. 'You know? Cuckoo-cuckoo crazy town?'

Elisa knocked. 'Tim, what's going on? I want to talk.'

'Um … just a second.' Tim checked through the peephole. In the long Dawn Star corridor, Elisa was looking down at her feet. As quietly as possible, Tim slid the door's chain-lock across – to be double sure.

She lifted her head at the noise, like a dog picking up a scent. 'Open it,' she said, through clenched teeth. 'Tim, do as I say. We don't have locked doors in this family.'

'Uh …'

'Tim!'

'Listen, Elisa,' he said. 'This will sound really naughty, and disrespectful, but … no.'

'I beg your pardon?'

'You've been overruled,' Dee added. 'You can't come in.'

'Elisa,' Tim said. 'Where … where is your mobile phone?'

'In my pocket,' she answered.

There was a pause – Tim and Dee both stared at one another. Then, with ferocious aggression, Elisa began kicking at the door. It fell open, stopping on the bronze chain, and her arm came through

195

the gap, swinging and clawing at them.

'Oh, this is a terrible evening,' Tim said, stepping away.

He sealed the door shut with some quickly created mega-glue, and then made a rope which they used to scale out of his window, escaping from the bedroom before she made it inside.

'That was really disturbing, seeing Elisa try to kill us,' Tim said, landing in the alley. He helped Dee down off the wall. 'Like, traumatic stuff.'

'It's character building, isn't it.' Dee shrugged. 'I'm sure you'll grow up to become a fine, well-rounded adult.'

'Yeah, kids are tough, resilient, right?'

'Well, God I hope so. Things I've seen online.'

'Ah,' he said, 'of course. That's why Elisa's been super cold recently – always on her phone, never caring where I am, what I do ...'

'Classic Mind Surfer.'

It wasn't too far to the Wilde Tech office – once they were there, it was just a quick teleport to safety. It was gone 7 p.m. now – the street lights had tinged the town in urban amber and Tim and Dee ran as fast as they could through the park, and across the drawbridge. The water, which seemed black, twinkled below them and Tim recalled the day he'd jumped it, almost exactly a week prior. They made it to the high street without incident.

The office they were headed for was in sight at the end of the road but, as they approached, Dee touched Tim's shoulder. A group of men in their early twenties had stopped up ahead of them. One of their faces was glowing a pale blue colour from the phone in his hand – his eyes turned to skeletal holes by the light. Then to their right, Tim noticed, inside a bright shop, a man slicing strips of greasy kebab from a rotating hunk of meat. His face twitched, warped and then completely relaxed. He then threw his legs over the counter and burst out, eyes locked on them, his knife as long as a sword.

'This way,' Dee said, dragging Tim towards an alleyway as strangers started in pursuit.

They trampled over some loose bin bags and scaled

a chain-link fence. However, when they arrived on the next street there was a long line of people queuing to get into the theatre. One by one nearly all of them turned – the ones who didn't, Tim reasoned, weren't IcoRama owners.

'This is just outrageous,' he said.

They bolted for a multistorey car park. The group behind them was now a crowd of perhaps thirty people, chasing with blank faces and lethal intent. A stitch pinched Tim's chest, his throat heaved with breath, as his feet thumped up the spiral tarmac road all the way to the roof.

As they arrived, however, a door up ahead swung open and another group, all shouldering each other, barged out. People were coming from all sides, some clambering over barriers, others literally stepping across the bonnets of cars, storming towards them like robots.

Like robots, Tim thought to himself.

He closed his eyes, slammed his imagination box on to the ground and pulled out a device about the size of an apple.

'What's that?' Dee said, her back pressed to his,

turning and turning, trying to face all of them at once.

'It's an EMP grenade,' he said. 'À la Squirrel Boarder.'

Tim tugged the pin out and the lever pinged off into the night. He threw it into the air as the possessed mob arrived.

Both he and Dee tensed, shielding themselves from incoming hands.

There was a loud blue explosion above – a lightning flash – and, flowing from them like ripples in a pond, street lights sparked, control boxes whirred down and every bulb in Glassbridge faded off.

And, most importantly of all, mobile phones were disabled.

By the remaining glow of the moon and stars, Tim and Dee looked around at the horde of strangers who were now sober, free and understandably bewildered.

'What the hell is going on?' one of them asked, glancing at the other confused faces.

'It's a long story,' Dee said.

'You all own IcoRama phones,' Tim shouted,

turning to address everyone. 'Smash them.'

That was all they had time to say because they needed to make it to Fredric's Glassbridge office before the electricity came back on.

After a short, spooky jog through the darkened town, they saw the building they were after. They went to the side entrance, noticing a discrete plaque mounted on the bricks with 'Wilde Tech' engraved in a fun font in the centre. The moment they fell inside, the lights flicked back on. Tim went straight to the rear room, using his freshly cooked key, to find the teleportation sphere.

They huddled close, clicked it and, after the hiss-pop and fuzzy feeling on their skin, reanimated in Wilde Tech's head office, in London.

Finally, they felt safe.

'I'm still not too keen on this sensation,' Dee said as Tim placed the blue counterpart sphere down on its pedestal.

They left the secret room and then went through to see if anyone was here.

'Fredric?' Tim said. But the office was empty. He glanced along the walls – the canvas of the Firestone

Turbo, the dragon poster, the floor-to-ceiling window overlooking the city.

'We are late, to be fair – we've taken our sweet time,' Dee said. 'He knows to meet us here though – he'll be along shortly I'm sure … Right, let's get to the bottom of this.'

She went straight to the computer and clicked it on, then sat on Fredric's large leather swivel chair.

'What are you doing?' Tim said, noticing Wilde Tech's familiar, colourful logo alight on the desktop.

'Samantha was right,' she explained, opening the internet browser and typing away. 'We need to get as much dirt on IcoRama as possible. Think about it logically, Tim, even with Fredric's help, who is going to believe us? And if anyone did believe us, the Mind Surfer has the power to change what people *think*. Or, if that fails, kill anyone he pleases. We need to *expose* whoever is behind this.'

'Yes,' Tim agreed, sighing. 'And Phil and Samantha? What if they're …' He couldn't say the words, but Dee knew what he meant.

'It is plausible they've been kidnapped, rather

than outright killed,' she said. 'Why else would the policemen have bundled them into the car?'

'But why kidnap them?'

'I dunno. Maybe they're more valuable alive?'

They did a number of searches online, reading all about IcoRama, looking for any possible connection, any clue, any link. It was originally a Canadian company which specialised in communication, firstly broadband, but last year they ventured into mobile phones.

'Owned by Smith and Olsen Limited,' Dee read. 'IcoRama was at the forefront of telecommunications during the early 2000s. However, following a fall in profits in recent years, the company was forced to go into administration.'

'What does that mean?' Tim said.

'It's when a business is proper rubbish,' Dee explained. 'And someone takes over and fixes it.'

'Oh.'

'Anyway,' she continued. 'There was a string of redundancies and, early last year, it seemed a certainty that IcoRama would cease operations forever. But, an eleventh-hour offer from investors DuskFire proved the lifeline the company needed. Now IcoRama commands the lion's share of the mobile-phone industry, with profits in the billions.'

'Investor, DuskFire,' Tim wondered aloud. 'That's what Samantha said in the car.'

Dee then started typing again, to search for more info, but the browser crashed. 'This is supposed to be a technology company,' she huffed.

Once more she keyed in a search and a load of documents appeared, all entitled 'DuskFire'.

'No,' Tim said. 'That's not the internet, see.' He pointed. 'Local results. These are on Fredric's computer.'

Nevertheless, she opened one up.

'DuskFire, a subsidiary of Wilde Tech Inc, was discreetly set up as a venture capital firm to allow us to invest in projects with no paper trail,' Tim read aloud. 'What the hell does this mean?'

Dee scrolled down.

'Therefore from August last year,' Tim read, 'Wilde Tech has been controller and majority shareholder of

IcoRama, without any unwanted interest from the press.'

'Wilde Tech?' Dee said, slowly turning to face him. 'Fredric is the investor. He *owns* IcoRama.'

Tim's breathing picked up a bit of pace as goosebumps drifted down his arms and across his shoulders. 'But, he said on the phone … he said he knew nothing about the company.'

'Well, then,' Dee added, 'Fredric Wilde is a liar.'

Chapter 15

On the top floor of Wilde Tech Inc's London offices, Tim and Dee sat in silence, both allowing what they'd read about Fredric to settle.

'So ... you think ... you think he has been working with Harriet this whole time?' Tim whispered. 'Why would he turn on her?'

'Not working with her,' Dee said. 'Maybe ... maybe *against* her. Of course. We've helped him destroy TRAD. It was the one organisation that would be able to stop him.'

'But, but ... I just can't ... no,' Tim said, shaking his head. He didn't want to believe it. 'There must be another explanation.'

'Was that why you couldn't create a working

teleportation sphere?' Dee said. 'Why we kept coming back to your room? Maybe, subconsciously, you knew? Or the information was finding its way to you ... So does that mean the fortune cookie was right? Granddad *is* innocent? Harriet too?'

Was it possible, Tim wondered. Were the clues there? Had he missed them? Or, worse, ignored them? He bit his fist, pacing across the room to the window. From the top of the building, the city seemed pretend, like a static backdrop in a game. He paused, then turned back. 'So what now?'

'He doesn't know that we know,' Dee said. 'Let's play dumb.'

'But ... let's say it's true ... won't he try to get rid of us? He knows we know about the phones.'

'Yes, but not that he's connected to them. It's the only way we'll get close enough to strike.'

'Strike?' Tim said. 'What do you mean?' Somehow he thought this revelation meant they'd need to come up with an entirely new plan.

'We're going ahead with it,' Dee said. 'We've got to stop him. What we need is a two-pronged attack.

We need to get a confession out of him, everything he knows, something to make it public. We'll ... we'll post it online, somewhere that he can't control. Let the world know.'

'And what's the other prong of this attack?' Tim asked.

'We have to destroy his underground desert facility.'

'That's where the imagination space is,' Tim said. 'But my castle ...'

'Think about it, that's also probably where his ... machine is ... What do they call it ... the mind board? That's probably his base of operations. The complex is huge – we've only seen a portion of it. What about all those hidden areas? Huh? All those labs ...'

'And Samantha and Phil?'

'Well, we can try and find them too, or after. Assuming they're not dead already.'

'You can say it in a softer way, Dee, you don't need—'

The familiar zipping whoosh sound came from the secret room and, a moment later, Fredric entered.

He then stepped in front of the window, silhouetted by the tiny specks of light – like stars – stretching off behind him. Tim swallowed – the stitch he had earlier when running somehow returned.

'I'm so pleased you guys made it,' Fredric said with concern that could be mistaken for genuine – Tim didn't know what to think.

He then suggested they come to Nevada with him, as they'd be 'safe' there. And so, wondering if this trip might be one-way, they followed Fredric across the globe in an instant.

Once they arrived in the control room of the desert facility, Fredric seemed to relax. Again Tim hoped, even wished, that there was some other reason for him denying involvement with IcoRama.

'If what you guys say is true,' Fredric said, pulling a stick of pink bubblegum from a silver packet, pointing with it as he spoke, 'then we'll need to tread carefully. If he is using phones, his reach could be … infinite.' He put it in his mouth, flicking the wrapper into the bin.

Shielding his eyes from the pseudo sunlight, Tim stepped to the window of the imagination space and stared past the treetops, sweeping to the right to see the long path across the grassy plain that led to his castle. He remembered the awesome afternoons, the hours he, Dee and Phil had spent in there – the rich world he watched flourish from his mind. Had it all been part of Fredric's trick, Tim wondered.

'Why don't you two head down there,' he said, noticing Tim's gaze. 'Take your mind off all this. Make a new roller coaster or something. Jetpacks maybe ... whatever you want. I've got some phone calls to make, things to clean up.'

'Why not,' Tim said, throwing his rucksack on to his back.

Downstairs, they clunked the door open and stepped inside. Tim pressed the thin metal reader on to his head and they strolled in among the palm trees where they were sure they were out of anyone's earshot. The light dimmed, the temperature dropped, Tim's mind subconsciously adding the weather of home to the formally majestic, tropical space.

'Why does he want us in here?' Dee asked. 'I don't like this at all.'

'Maybe, because while I'm wearing this,' Tim tapped the metal reader, 'he knows where I am.'

'It takes data readings,' Dee said. 'But … he can't track me.'

'Exactly.'

Tim led her through the woodland, past the glowing butterflies and dancing dandelion seeds – the barbershop birds were singing a sombre song now, as though they knew something had changed. They arrived at the base of Tim's castle. He looked up, past his creation, and now really noticed the edges of the room – the metal struts above that reminded him of an aircraft hangar. The whole place felt more fake than ever, like a movie set. On the long garden table, one of the zappers Tim had been using to fine-tune things was waiting. He passed it to Dee.

'Take this – use it to blast open any locked doors,' he told her. 'If Samantha and Phil are here, they're probably in the lower rooms. Find them.'

Dee had said it was possible they'd been brought

here, perhaps to be used as a bargaining tool if needs be. It was just a theory, but well worth exploring. They had to ensure they were safe before attempting to destroy the place.

'And if I do?' she asked.

'Get them out and make for the surface,' Tim said.

'Can't we just teleport?'

'The only places you can get a signal are the control room and high up,' Tim said. 'Sadly we're just going to have to escape the old-fashioned way. I'll meet you up top, once I've dealt with Fredric.'

'How are you going to do that?' Dee said.

'I'm going to have a civilised conversation with him, get him to confess, and I'm going to secretly film it and, then, when we're high enough for signal, post the footage online.'

'Clever.'

'Two-pronged attack,' Tim said. 'You save them, I'll do the rest.'

'How will you escape afterwards?'

'I'll ... I'll work something out.'

'But—'

'Just go.'

Tim thickened the foliage at the top of the trees near the high viewing window, just in case Fredric was looking down, as Dee made for the door. She snuck out of sight and Tim, now alone, sighed to himself.

He then created a camera and microphone interwoven into his shirt. Feeling the warm plastic against his chest reminded him of Phil, but he couldn't get distracted by sentiment.

The plan was relatively simple: find out Fredric's involvement in all this and then, if necessary, destroy this entire complex with the imagination space – once everyone had got out safely. He'd need to keep the reader and remotely conjure unfathomable amounts of fire, or something equally as devastating, in here.

Really, Tim thought, as he placed his rucksack on the long table, there were *three* prongs to this attack . . .

It was going to be tricky. In fact, he realised, growing more doubtful by the minute, it was pretty much impossible to do this alone; he would somehow need to be in two places at the same time . . .

A few minutes later, Fredric appeared near the

entrance of the imagination space and called him over.

'Tim,' he yelled – it echoed. 'Come up to the control room, we need to talk.'

Yes we do, Tim thought. He hesitated, looking through the ferns, past the flower beds, all the way to the castle. 'All right, just a sec.'

Glancing back, Tim saw Fredric standing, waiting for him.

As he approached, Tim reached into his pocket and was pleased to find the metal reader. The camera he had made was recording, its lens imbedded in his shirt button. He pictured what the footage might look like – shot low, juddering and amateur, but good enough.

'Where's Dee?' Fredric asked, checking over Tim's shoulder.

'She's just . . . she's just gone up to the castle,' he lied. 'Want me to get her?'

'No, no. She can't go far, can she?'

As they arrived in the control room, Fredric turned to Tim and smiled. He pulled out a seat and placed it next to his desk, then slumped down into his swivel chair. 'Where's your imagination box?' he asked, noticing Tim wasn't wearing his reader hat or carrying his rucksack.

'I left it on the table outside the castle,' Tim said, rubbing the back of his neck. 'Anyway, what's … what's our next move?'

They were sitting in a soft orange light, a distorted rectangular beam glowing from the imagination space. Their shadows were long on the wall to Tim's right – the angle and his height made Fredric's loom above, halfway to the ceiling.

'You tell me, man,' he said. 'You've done most of the hard work. So, when did you figure it out?'

'Figure what out?' Tim was testing the water – there was still room for doubt. A place in his heart still wanted Fredric to have a reasonable excuse for everything.

'When did you realise it was the phones?'

'Oh. Dee told me she'd been playing on her IcoRama in the bath,' Tim said. 'Her mum told her she couldn't, in case she dropped it in the water. Like the very first man who chased me. He leapt into the river then he snapped out of it. Broken phone. The Mind Surfer's first mistake.'

'Ah, yeah,' Fredric said. 'Of course ... the suited dude. On reflection, what a strange choice of target for whoever *is* behind this.'

'What do you mean?' Tim asked.

'Come on, a man with a bowler hat and a black umbrella? Doesn't that just scream secret agent? Almost too obvious, isn't it?'

Only now that he said it did Tim remember the morning clearly. The concussion had wiped the memory of what the man who chased him through the market had been wearing. He nodded, feeling a strange sadness in his gut – a sensation similar to the fall of his roller coaster. Now he was sure. One hundred per cent sure. Dee had been right.

Fredric Wilde was a liar.

'What's wrong?' he said, chewing on his bubblegum.

'I never told you he had a bowler hat and umbrella,' Tim said.

Staring into those blue-grey eyes, Tim saw through – past the gloss and promises – to the truth inside. It was like looking down into the screen of an IcoRama phone.

For a long while, Fredric sat in silence, squinting briefly. He rubbed his earlobe then looked around the control room. Somehow, Tim managed to keep a poker face. The fact he was recording this conversation made him sweat – a drip tickled his hairline and he scratched it away.

Fredric leant back in his chair and blew a large bubble, which popped loud. All the while he smiled. All the while enjoying himself.

'It's you,' Tim said. 'You're the Mind Surfer.'

And then Fredric tapped the desk with his knuckle and stood, his shadow riding past the ceiling now, curving over.

'Well done, Tim,' he said, turning his palms, exposing them to the warm, artificial sunlight. 'You got me.'

Chapter 16

The control room was silent. Tim didn't really know what to say next – he was surprised how ready Fredric was to admit it.

'So it's true. You've been controlling people?'

'I'm not a fan of the pseudonym,' Fredric said. 'But, yeah, long story short, yeah, man. I have. Now that you know, you are aware that I've got to file you away, right?' He calmly removed his black zapper from his pocket. 'Firstly, put the reader on the table.'

Tim did as he said. The metal crown clinked on to the wood in the centre of the long, stretched patch of light. His mouth was dry, his heart thudding audibly against his ribs, making the camera beneath his shirt lift and drop.

'Farewell, Tim,' Fredric added, taking aim. 'It's been a blast.'

'Wait,' Tim said. He knew that whatever happened it was crucial he got a full, comprehensive confession on tape. 'At least . . . at least tell me why.'

Fredric pouted, then lowered the zapper. 'Hey, no harm in that. What do you want to know?'

'None of it makes any sense. I . . . I just don't understand.'

'Right,' Fredric said. 'From the top. I was there, in Glassbridge. I listened to Eisenstone's "There is a box" speech, when he explained the concept. So exciting, so revolutionary. Genius really. A gadget that can create anything . . . You know what I felt, sitting there at the back, hearing about the technology? I felt *terrified*.'

'Why?'

'I built my entire career – my entire life, man – on *selling* things to people. That's how our society works, Tim. Consumer capitalism is the reason you're alive, it's the reason for western civilisation as we know it. Can you *imagine* what would happen if everyone had an imagination box? Money would become obsolete, overnight. And then what?'

'So, you created the mind board?'

'Yeah, I designed a device that could transmit thoughts into other people's heads. Something you know well ... Clarice Crowfield and Professor Whitelock did a very similar thing with you. On the shoulders of giants. That's why I leased this facility from TRAD. It had to be well out of the way. And on top of that, working with them helped get me close – I could see the agency's weak points.'

'Why mobile phones?'

'I quickly realised I would need a network of devices that would send signals to people's brains. IcoRama 2020 phones were in development, but the business was struggling, so I purchased the company and modified the design slightly. I started small, obviously, getting people to do silly things, for my own entertainment. At first people resisted. It caused riots. But then I refined it and it functioned like a charm. People ran to the shops to panic-buy carrots, various products, even *more phones*. No matter what happened with Eisenstone's technology, I knew I could get people to keep buying things.'

'Seems a bit over the top to me, controlling everyone just to flog stuff – quite a risk?'

'The brazen, the audacious, these are the crimes that no one notices. Steal some candy and you'll land yourself in all kinds of trouble, but walk out confidently with a flat-screen TV ... no one cares, man ...' Fredric was still smiling.

Tim was squinting, his brow furrowed. 'And you killed people who got too close to the truth?'

'Come on, man, the greater good?' Fredric shrugged. 'What I've done, protecting our way of life, protecting commerce, industry, protecting the very notion of capitalism – the foundation of our world? The imagination box is a device that appeals to the worst in us – it appeals to greed, the desire for *more*. Unlimited unearned stuff, for free? If it became a household tool, society would *crumble*. People wouldn't go to their jobs, farms would shut down, factory floors would be homes for rats and weeds ...'

Had it always been a good thing, Tim thought

to himself, being able to create everything he'd ever wanted and more? Perhaps not. But that didn't justify these drastic measures.

'Times change,' Tim said. 'You can't uninvent things.'

'That's true, and I'd be lying if I said the technology isn't awesome. But a nuclear explosion is awesome too.'

'So, you're scared of change,' Tim said. 'That's an old man's problem.'

'It's a wise man's problem.'

'But that still doesn't explain *my* role in all of this? Why steal my imagination box?'

'This is where my plan got innovative, elegant,' Fredric said. He now stepped completely out of the light, pacing a short distance to another work station, where he perched. 'You understand that the Technology, Research and Defence agency like to sniffle around, getting their nose in people's business. They developed their own mind board, a prototype. You saw it. They would, inevitably, have discovered what I was up to. And then they would have pulled the plug, had me put in prison. There was also speculation online, conspiracy theorists – people were taking notice of what I was doing. Harriet herself had begun an investigation. So I needed to get rid of them for good, cut off the head of the snake. That's where you came in, Tim. I needed a keen individual, someone malleable, someone yearning for adventure.'

Nodding, Tim remembered how true it had been.

'And who better than you? You could help me learn even more about the technology, help me discover ways to block it. *All* the answers are in your brain, after all. So I stole your box, got *you* to come to *me*. It had to seem like you were figuring it all out yourself. Then you jumped through each hoop even more obediently than I had hoped.'

'What about Eisenstone?'

'He's too smart, that guy. He was gonna make the imagination box work for everyone – it was a matter of time. I had to nip that in the bud. Framing him seemed obvious. I mean, as good as the mind board was, it was only ever a precautionary measure. It was hardly sustainable.'

It was funny to think that if it wasn't for this part of his scheme, Fredric may well have got away with it. Tim might have missed the rest, overlooked the other niggles and concerns he had. Framing Eisenstone though, Tim thought, was Fredric's biggest error.

'And Harriet?'

'Innocent,' Fredric said. 'Collateral damage.'

'But ... but what about the emails I downloaded from her computer?' Tim said. 'I read them. *She* arranged for the box to be stolen, she wanted to kill me.'

'The emails you *down*loaded?' Fredric raised an eyebrow. 'Come on, man, think it through. No, Tim, you *up*loaded them. You *planted* that evidence.'

Tim felt sick, he felt used. 'And you guided Dee straight to my imagination box,' he said, remembering how she just had a 'feeling' where it was. 'You were controlling her the whole time.'

'That's right, and I told you, via her, to create Harriet's password.' He lifted an arm, proud of himself. 'There's *no way* I could have hacked into that computer without your help. So, thank you.'

Tim sighed. There had been times when he'd thought that *he* was to blame for all of this. It had turned out to be an awfully appropriate way to feel.

'You're a microscopic cog in my well-thought-out plan,' Fredric added. 'No TRAD, no one left to stop me.'

'Well,' Tim said, pointing to himself, copying Fredric's trademark eyebrow lift. 'Me?'

'Sure.' Fredric gave a condescending nod. 'I've locked the imagination space. Dee's going nowhere.'

Managing to hide it well, Tim knew that to be untrue. She'd already left.

'Samantha and Phil are in cuffs downstairs,' Fredric said. 'I kept them alive to have a bit of leverage when I was struggling to catch you guys. Didn't even need it. You came here *willingly*. It's almost too easy, Tim … Anyway, I'd have liked to have done some more testing, but you've spoiled that now.'

Dee appeared in the doorway, behind Fredric. Tim was overwhelmed with joy to see Phil on her shoulder and Samantha by her side.

'All that's left for me to do is tie up these loose ends,' Fredric said, lifting the zapper.

'Freeze!' Dee yelled, pointing hers at his back.

'Oh,' he said. 'You've found the prisoners.'

'Put it down on the ground,' Dee demanded. '*Slowly*.'

Tim smirked from his seat. Astonishingly, the plan had gone better than expected. The tables had finally turned. Tim was in control for the first time.

'Sure thing,' Fredric said.

But then, in one swift motion, he leant back, dodging the beam Dee instinctively fired, and shot the zapper in her hands. A flash – it turned to air.

Tim panicked, shuffling back – he was completely vulnerable again. His brain was jumbled – he felt like running, but there was nowhere to go. Now the situation was out of his grasp and a uniquely hopeless dread – usually found only in the darkest of nightmares – drove through him.

'Now, *you* freeze,' Fredric said, spitting out his gum and facing Tim. 'Where were we? Oh yeah, I was gonna do this.'

In a desperate surge of raw horror Tim watched Fredric lift his aim and shoot the zapper at his chest. Tim was aware of the hot beam hitting his sternum, his flesh, bone and blood disconnecting, spreading away from the centre of his torso. The clean destruction zipped towards his face, down to his legs, to his fingers and toes.

A short screaming sound, maybe the howl of wind or the crack of whip, and then Tim's very thoughts were gone.

No white light, no flare of life.

There was simply nothing.

Chapter 17

Now there was a lot of noise in the control room. Phil had ended up on the floor, standing beside the wheel of a swivel chair. The monkey saw Dee had taken cover and was crouched behind a work station in the corner, her knees tucked to her chest. Fredric was on the other side, taking pot shots with the zapper. Objects above Dee's head – a lamp, a computer monitor, a mug – disappeared, one by one, with a crack.

Samantha had also ducked down near the door. She was shouting, telling Dee to run, or something like that. It was all a haze – a surreal, incandescent flurry.

All these sounds, but Phil couldn't hear a thing. There was nothing but a haunting wail in his ears, his vision jittering; he was gripped by the shock of what Fredric had done. How quickly and callously he had shot Tim. How, without a flicker of regret, he had taken his best friend, his creator, away.

When he was captured Phil had seen the restricted areas in the belly of this complex – the computers, the readers and the huge mind board, exactly like TRAD's prototype, only larger. Now, calming down, he nodded to himself, watching the carnage unfold. The anger and grief and outrage motivated him. All at once, he knew what he had to do: Fredric and this entire place simply had to go.

Tim had been right, the monkey thought, perhaps creativity *is* the best therapy. So he scurried on to the leg of the swivel chair, up on to the cushioned fabric and then leapt to the desk above. At his side, out of focus, Fredric strolled casually towards Dee, about to finish the job. Phil stepped in the other direction, across the table, approaching the reader. He wrestled it upright, then carefully pulled the thin metal legs apart and gently bent the ends on to his temples.

Phil looked across the control room, through the

viewing window, into the vast imagination space – the pseudo sun still glowed orange, warm on his skin. To date, of course, only Tim had been able to use the technology. Now that he thought about it, Phil was surprised no one had considered letting him have a go. After all, Tim had imagined the monkey. It wasn't unthinkable that he'd possess the requisite attributes.

In fact, Phil thought to himself, it was jolly likely.

His head made contact with the small plastic pads on the reader. There was a tingling on his fur as he closed his eyes and pictured – as vividly as Tim always did – something that could appear in the space next door and sort out this whole fiasco. Yes, he had something suitable in mind.

Phil scrunched his face and imagined. A second later there was a low, loud *THHWHUUUM* sound and, in an instant, the control room was filled with a dim blue light.

Fredric stopped dead, lowering his zapper and turning to the window. The imagination space was full, floor to ceiling, wall to wall, with water. Cascading patterns painted everything around

Phil – it felt like they were looking through the porthole of a submarine. Fredric's head whipped to the side, staring down at the monkey.

'My God,' he said, wrapped in astonishment. 'You . . . *you* can use it too?'

He stepped closer, seeming to forget about Dee and Samantha. Phil scurried to the edge of the desk. The huge space looked like a forgotten city – the tops of trees, pathways, roller coaster and plains were eerie and still beneath the water. It was crystal clear, like the ocean surrounding a Caribbean island – and yet the castle at the far side was barely visible, a mere darkened shape now. Even the clearest liquid is opaque at such distances.

'I mean, well done, Phil,' Fredric said. 'Sadly, I doubt this is gonna save you. While this is impressive, I think you could have been a little more imaginative than just water.'

'Poppycock,' the monkey replied, smiling like Fredric might. 'I am afraid, good sir, it is not *just* water.'

There was a deep, ominous rumble as a vast presence,

just a shadow at first, then a mass of *something*, swam past the window. 'W-what? What was that?'

'I have conjured up what I suspect is the deadliest predator on earth,' Phil said, unable to hide his pride. 'I have created . . . bear-sharks.'

Unsure exactly how many he'd made, Phil stared into the immense aquarium: he counted two, no three, no five, whale-sized monsters. Maybe more. They had the broad muzzles of bears, with the sleek length of a great white shark. Large, substantial legs were tucked flat to their bodies as the creatures swam – their brown fur rippled almost beautifully.

'Bear-sharks?' Fredric said, frowning.

'Bear-sharks,' Phil confirmed.

'Still,' Fredric added, hypnotised by the sight of them. 'They're in there and we're in here. I'm afraid to say, little monkey dude, that this is still the end of the road for you.'

He turned and pointed the zapper at Phil – the marine patterns flowing across them both – but, behind him, one of the mammoth creations came swimming at an astonishing speed towards the window. The entire control room shook – like an earthquake – from the impact. Fredric lost his balance, swaying, as a few thin streams of water spurted through fresh cracks in the glass.

The second time one of them attacked, a large triangular shard fell out and a torrent came bursting into the room. It swept Fredric from his feet, and picked up chairs and tables, washing them to the wall. He tried again to fire the zapper but, now wet, it wouldn't work. Realising what was happening, Fredric seemed to panic and made for the exit. The moment he was outside, the two mechanical doors to the control room slammed shut, sealing Phil, Dee and Samantha inside.

Dee had clambered out from her hiding place, now wading, the cold rising to her waist.

'Phil,' she said, letting the monkey climb from the desk, up her arm and on to her shoulder. The strip light above them had become a strobe, flickering madly.

Samantha was at the door, yanking at the switch and elbowing the handle. It was no use.

'It's locked,' she said, barging with her shoulder.

Again, there was a loud impact somewhere nearby. Although Phil couldn't see it, he could feel that those huge beasts were destroying the place. Luckily, they'd given up on breaking though the window, for now.

However, the rough water – like a choppy ocean for the tiny monkey – was still rising fast, now near Dee's armpits.

'What are we going to do?' Samantha yelled, turning, striding.

'I suspect we are going to die,' Dee replied. She was clearly in shock, her voice slower than normal – stunned by what she'd seen.

As Samantha got to the other side of the room, there was a whack on the door, making her flinch. Then another. And another. It was rhythmic. Something on the other side was bashing, again and again, trying to break in.

'Yep,' Dee added, calm as a cucumber. 'We're either going to drown, or be eaten by bear-sharks. Not sure which.' The banging on the metal continued. 'It sounds like the latter probably, which I suppose *is* the lesser of two evils. Phil, why are your bear-sharks so hostile?'

'I needed to imagine the most deadly and destructive animal on the planet,' the monkey replied, clinging on to her neck for balance. 'If I am entirely honest, I did it quite quickly and with perhaps less than an ideal amount of forethought. So if this decision does precede our demise, then I wholeheartedly apologise.'

Her warm skin was comforting – a far cry from the chilled spray in the air. He looked up and noticed her cheeks were glistening with tears. It was a bewildering sight – he'd assumed Dee was too tough, too hard to cry, even at a time like this. And yet she spoke as though this was just another day, betrayed only by her body's reaction to the loss of her best friend.

'You should have created them to be friendly to us,' she said.

'Yes, perhaps next time I will.'

The water had just passed her shoulders, splashing to Phil's knees, so she stepped on to a chair. It was perhaps another thirty seconds before the level would be at the ceiling. 'I don't think there will be a next time,' Dee said, 'as it sounds like one of them is about to come through there.'

With one final thump, the door came off its hinges and some, but not all, of the water sloshed out, tugging them along.

Holding on to the fixed desk, Dee and Samantha yelled, Phil too, expecting imminent death. But, in the doorway, instead of a giant bear-shark, there was a person, clutching a fire-axe. He was wearing a red-chequered shirt and a black rucksack. He lifted his head.

'T-Timothy?' Phil said. 'What ... what the devil is going on here?'

'Tim,' Dee yelled, scrambling, tripping, swimming to hug him. She arrived and squeezed. 'What's happening? Fredric ... he shot you. He zapped you right up.'

'Yes,' Tim said. 'He did.'

There was a pause. Samantha, Dee and Phil were all staring at him. 'Well, explain yourself,' Dee snapped.

'I … I feared he would zap me away once he'd confessed. What I needed was to transmit a video of everything he told me, via the facility's internal network, to this.' Tim held up a small USB memory stick, containing the incriminating footage. 'It meant I had to be in two places at the same time.'

'But that is surely not possible,' Phil said.

Tim glanced across the rising water, to the window.

'You … you imagined *yourself*?' Samantha asked, shaking her head. 'So there were two Tims? Like a clone?'

'Bingo,' Tim said. 'Old Cloney's gone now though, which is a shame because he was all right. Handsome.'

'By anyone's estimations it is good to see you, sir,' Phil added, before finding his way into Tim's top pocket. 'Terrific hustle. Telling us could have spared some distress, however.'

'It was a last-minute plan. All's well that ends well.' It was a relieving moment for Tim, being reunited with the others. Even though they were far from safe, he still felt lightly satisfied with this limited success. He also silently hoped that his clone's disappearance wasn't too traumatic for him. Poor guy.

'Now just the small matter of escaping and getting that confession online,' Samantha said.

Nodding, Tim asked, 'What the *hell* is going on with all this water?'

'It is not *just* water,' Phil said.

The monkey then explained what had happened, that he too was able to use the technology.

'That's ... that's cool,' Tim said.

Was it cool? Initially, Tim felt something fundamental had changed. A shift in tides. He'd always taken quiet pride in his abilities, but now he wasn't the only one. He wasn't special.

'I would not wish you to feel at all besmirched by this revelation,' Phil said. 'I am, after all, a creation of yours. Credit where it is due.'

Although a strange thought, the monkey was right – all this was ultimately Tim's doing.

However, like the others, he also felt that Phil's first creations were somewhat lacking in practicality. 'Yeah, anyway, about these bear-sharks,' Tim said. 'I am impressed, well done and everything. It's just ...

as awesome as they are . . . I can't see how they're going to help . . .'

'Will you all stop rustling my fur about the bear-sharks,' Phil said. 'Fredric has gone, has he not? They have bought us some time, at the very least.'

'Can we get out that way?' Dee asked, looking over Tim's shoulder. The light above was fizzing, flickering now faster than ever, the cold water rising again.

'Nope,' Tim said. 'Fredric's sealed all the doors. Hence the axe.'

'So you came in here so we can drown together?' Dee said. 'That's sweet.'

'No.' Tim grabbed the metal crown reader from the table then waded across the control room to the main console. 'I've got a plan.'

He shook his head at all the complex dials and buttons – half of them were submerged. Near the top was a protruding section with a few wires sticking out – it was labelled 'Reader Calibration Station'.

'Heh,' Phil said. 'Rhymes.'

'What are you doing?' Samantha asked.

'The reader won't work because it's wet,' Tim said,

238

placing it on his head, remembering when Fredric had explained all this. He then tugged the cable towards his ear. 'If I plug it in, and press this switch, I think it'll reset it. Recalibrate it. Then I can imagine something to get rid of all this water.'

'Superb,' Phil said.

Tim clicked in the plug, then flicked two switches, hearing it power-up. The final part of the process was a red button, beneath one of those safety covers. With a wet finger, he reached out and pressed it, hoping that—

Thud.

Sparks and a terrible sound. The reader roared on his head, sending shards of razor agony down his spine. A guttural scream, which Tim realised was his, echoed around him.

The next thing he knew, he was on his back, floating in the water, staring up at the flashing light above, his vision rotating like a fairground tunnel. And a moment later he was sinking asleep, having the most vivid dream about home.

Chapter 18

Concerned voices faded in over the static hiss in the flooded control room. '... hear us? Tim?' Loud and clear now. 'Tim, wake up. Can you hear us?'

With a flinch, Tim sat up, his feet sinking to the floor. He checked over his shoulder, confused. 'What happened?'

'The control station, it exploded,' Samantha said. 'The reader is fried.'

A hollow pain behind Tim's eyes, like a sore tooth, eased and he composed himself.

'Are you OK?' Dee asked.

'Yeah, I ... I think so.' He rubbed his temples. 'I feel a bit sick, but I'm all right.'

This was only half true – Tim could tell that

something was wrong with his body. He could feel it in his bones.

'Another plan, perhaps?' Phil said.

The water was still rising as Tim waded to the window – it glowed blue and a thick stream continued to pump through the hole. He was shivering. 'There's a ... a service hatch on the ceiling of the imagination space.'

Dee looked up through the cracked glass, narrowing her eyes. 'I can't see it?'

'Trust me,' Tim said. 'It's there, it's just a long way away.'

'So ...' Dee said.

'We're going to have to swim,' Samantha added, removing her jacket.

Phil then suggested, with a tone of fear in his voice, that Tim use his imagination box, which he still had strapped to his back, to make breathing apparatus for everyone. Or, even better, some teleportation spheres. However, like the metal reader, Tim's hat was soaking wet and would be useless until it dried.

Everyone prepared themselves as best they could. Samantha took the axe.

'Ready?' she asked, looking between Tim and Dee. They both nodded, holding on to the desk. 'All right . . . three, two, *one*.'

Grunting, she swung it into the glass, smashing it completely. The room flooded – right to the ceiling – in two seconds flat. After getting thrashed around in the loud rapids, they took their last gasps of air from the lighting recesses and then dived down. Everything became quiet, muffled – a blunt ache arrived in Tim's ears from the pressure.

Samantha went first, followed by Dee. Then Tim grabbed the viewing-window frame and pulled himself through. Above, below and ahead of him was cold, sea-deep water – so much that he couldn't see the edges of the imagination space. As he swam a clumsy breaststroke, he looked down at all he'd created – castle, forest, roller coaster and more – now sunken, like a shipwreck. He pictured all those rooms, the thousands of items, desires – floating now, drowned and broken.

Up ahead, there was a high-pitched scream – light silvery bubbles flowed from Samantha's mouth and rose quickly.

A mammoth shadow passed below. Tim's stomach sank. He kept kicking and kicking upwards as another huge shape moved to his right. Swimming in a line, heading diagonally towards the centre of the high ceiling, they were being circled.

Legs burning, Tim's heart pounded, tightening his ribs as his vision started to shroud.

He was swimming so hard that only when he bashed his head on the metal did he realise they had arrived. Feeling absurdly vulnerable, Tim ducked down again and shimmied over to the door, his body dangling below him, like bait from a hook. The hatch had a large circular handle which he grabbed on to. It was stuck.

Samantha and Dee joined in, all tugging, wide-eyed, desperate for air, seconds from death. Tugging, tugging, tugging ... Finally, it squeaked and scraped round, then lifted away. They poked their heads out above the rippling surface, all heaving and gasping.

Tim raised his chest so Phil too could take a few urgent breaths.

He swam aside and let Dee and Samantha through to the service ladder which led up a narrow shaft, connecting the imagination space to the desert above.

The last thing Tim saw, as he pulled himself up from the dark water, was one of the monsters rising and snapping for his feet. With a splash and a yelp, he got out just in time, feeling the spray from its roar lurch up, echoing through the service tunnel. Above them was a perfect circle of daylight, like the rim of a well.

On the surface, atop the underground facility below them, they got their bearings. Tim leant forwards, catching his breath, the blazing desert already starting to dry him – wet dirt and sand muddied his hands and jeans. The sky was the deepest blue, a couple of vultures circling up ahead of them. Sunshine split and flared through his stinging eyes. Jutting high behind was a large metal antenna, covered in satellites and aerials, taller than the biggest pylon Tim had ever seen. It's obviously what sends the signals to IcoRama phones, he thought.

They began running down the steep hill, clambering over rocks which were almost too hot to touch. Before them, across a large expanse of desert, peppered with cracked shrubs and stones, was an airfield. A white, personal plane was parked at the end of the runway. Beyond that, distant, faded mountains met the horizon.

Tim tried to get his imagination box to work – some teleportation spheres would be very helpful – but irritatingly the soaked reader still wasn't functioning at all.

'We can't wait for your hat to dry,' Dee said. 'We'll just have to steal Fredric's Learjet.'

'Fine by me,' Samantha added. 'I can fly that thing.'

She was right, Tim thought, they had to get away from here as quickly as possible. Phil's bear-sharks were probably taking care of one prong of their plan by destroying the entire facility. Now, they had to upload that confession on to the internet.

They reached the bottom of the incline and, after losing his footing and stumbling to his knees, Tim looked back. He saw the tall rocks behind them – the incredibly large imagination space was inside there, hidden away underground.

But then, Tim's legs tingled with the power of a seismic shudder. Pieces of grit vibrated on nearby boulders, a distorted strain of metal came from below.

'What was that?' he asked.

There was an explosion of dust, rubble and muddy water, and a hole appeared in the side of the steep hill. Behind them, a tidal wave came thundering down and, as if that wasn't bad enough, galloping amid the torrent was a herd of extremely angry-looking bear-sharks.

'Phil,' Tim said, sighing with every kind of exhaustion. 'Why are they amphibious?'

'Because they are BEAR-sharks,' the monkey answered.

'It does make sense,' Dee added.

They all bolted for the plane.

At the airfield they ducked into one of the hangars. The creatures weren't far behind, eating, smashing and causing every flavour of chaos around them. There was a short lull in the carnage, so they ran, bent at the waist, along the runway, towards Fredric's private jet.

Across the flat section of desert Tim spotted a large grey door in the side of the mountain begin to lift.

'They're leaving the facility,' Tim said. 'No sign of Fredric. We need to—'

They stopped. One of the beasts had rolled a jeep on to its roof and was mauling the underside. Then it noticed them. Tim saw its enraged face, snarling like a bear, stretched like a shark, a piece of wheel hanging from its lower jaw.

'They do look proper scary,' Tim said.

'Thank you,' Phil replied.

It came thumping towards them. They ran, making it to a small outbuilding, Tim at the rear.

'No, no, no,' he screamed, looking over his shoulder.

The bear-shark pounced heavily towards him, throwing him inside. Skidding, he rolled over, ears ringing, to see its wide skull stuck in the doorway, which splintered as it writhed. It growled and snorted, rows of razor-sharp teeth snapped together, hot breath on Tim's clothes. In fact, it was *really* hot. They all watch, transfixed, as it lowered its head and puffed up its chest, sucking in a gulp of air. Then it opened its mouth with an almighty rumble and thick fire roared out.

'What?' Tim said as he threw himself over a table.

Samantha tipped it for cover. Dee hit the ground just in time. The flames were blasting above, steam and smoke stinging Tim's skin. 'Phil,' he shouted over the noise. 'Why can they breathe fire?!'

'Frankly, Timothy,' the monkey yelled, 'I am as surprised as you.'

The attack eased and Tim peeked over. Embers crackled throughout the room. The animal was still wedged, so they clambered out of the window as it prepared for another go.

They were on the home straight now – there was nothing between them and the plane.

'We've only gone and done it,' Dee said, running by Tim's side. 'Got the confession on tape, pretty much destroyed that place. Those sharky bears will surely have done enough damage.'

Tim looked back to the facility – the tall antenna

was falling now, being torn to bits by the beasts.

They ran and ran until, when only a few strides from their escape, the plane simply disappeared. Tim tripped, almost reaching out to grab what was no longer there. For a second he thought it might have been a mirage. But an American voice from behind said, 'Not on my watch.'

It was Fredric, zapper in hand, approaching from the thick shadow of the nearby hangar, turned relatively black by the afternoon's glare. He was relentless.

'No one's going anywhere,' he said. 'Tim, take the reader off your head and throw it on to the ground.'

Realising he had no other option, Tim did as he said and watched Fredric, without hesitation, zap it away.

'Now, the rucksack.'

It thumped to the ground.

Zip-pop and it too was gone, just a slight haze of desert dust where it had been.

This moment saddened Tim beyond measure. That imagination box, its infinite uses aside, had a great deal of sentimental value. He had also told Eisenstone he would bring it home safely. Another promise broken.

'Now, *once again*, where were we?' Fredric said, his trainers crunching on the pebbles as he strolled towards Samantha. 'And why is Tim back?'

Tim gave him a quick summary.

Fredric seemed to admire the illusion. 'That's actually quite smart,' he said.

They all shared a silence.

'You killed my husband,' Samantha said, defeated, completely out of ideas, just speaking from the heart. 'You murdered him.'

'You lied to me, you destroyed my imagination box,' Tim added. 'You had me chased. You made my own family attempt to kill me. You had me send my friend to prison.'

'He also shot your clone with a zapper,' Phil added.

'Yeah, that too.'

'And ... and you led me to believe you'd figure out a way for me to have my own imagination box,' Dee said. Fredric frowned. 'Yeah, I know, it's not as bad as the others,' she admitted. 'Tim sort of said my one already – about Granddad.'

'None of this is on,' Phil said. 'It is just not cricket.'

'I made you a car,' Tim added, still running over all the bad stuff Fredric had done.

'Yeah, a bear-shark ate that,' Fredric said.

'Sorry,' Phil said. Dee glared at him. 'Oh no,' he added. 'Maybe I am not sorry.'

Strangely, at a time like this, in all probability minutes from death, Tim was able to think clearly. The overriding thought, he discovered, was an odd curiosity about Fredric and all he had done.

'One thing I don't get,' Tim wondered. 'Why build an imagination space for me to play in? I mean, despite all the manipulation, megalomania and murder, you seemed . . . all right.'

Fredric laughed. 'I've made a substantial living out of selling technology,' he said. 'You learn quickly that you can take whatever you please from people, so long as they think they're getting what they want.'

'Then why did you keep me around after I'd served my purpose?' Tim asked. 'After TRAD was shut down, after Eisenstone was in prison?'

'Dude, I like you – this isn't easy for me. Plus there were too many unanswered questions. I needed to know more about the technology, ultimately to find a way to stop it becoming mainstream. Or, at the very least, find a way to make it commercial. You know, in case the mobiles didn't work. But the success I had with IcoRama phones was *phenomenal*. I could take over anyone – more than ninety-nine per cent of the time the mind control worked. And when it didn't, it was down to technical faults. Younger brains were a little harder to crack, but I had ways round it. We developed a game to maximise exposure – dunno if you've heard of it, Squirrel Boarder.'

'Oh, you monster,' Dee said. 'That's it – that's my thing. That's the worst one.'

'However, there was one fully functioning IcoRama out there on the network and its user's mind was impenetrable,' Fredric went on. 'And who owned that phone?'

Tim smiled.

'You did,' Fredric added. 'I just couldn't make it affect you. I needed to know why.'

'His phone was fake, duh. He made it in his imagination box,' Dee said, squinting, shaking her head, clearly still upset about the Squirrel Boarder thing. 'Keep up.'

Fredric glanced at the ground, then looked back. 'Oh yeah. Obvious now you say it.'

'It's over,' Tim said, staring up into those light eyes. 'You must see that? What *possible* sense is there in killing us now?'

'It's . . . I'm sorry . . . but I've come this far . . . It's for the best. I wish you guys could understand.' Fredric stepped to Dee and lifted the zapper.

This was it, Tim thought, sighing on his knees. No imagination box, no one to help them for miles. It was the end. They had lost.

Dee turned to the side. 'Goodbye,' she whispered, with a casual wave.

Tim closed his eyes.

There was a flash.

Silence.

When he looked back a brick wall had appeared in front of Dee. 'What the?' Fredric said, confused.

Tim then calmly rose to his feet.

Fredric took aim, but Tim simply lifted his palm and the zapper melted, landing at their feet in a twisted, steamy glob.

'What's going on?' Fredric yelled.

Pointing with his other arm, his face straight with concentration, Tim watched handcuffs appear, as if from nowhere, around Fredric's wrists. Then prison bars, carved from desert rock, jutted from the ground, all around him. Within two seconds, Fredric was lifted high in a cage, tied, taped, bound, chained and restrained in every way Tim could imagine. A one-man jail, custom built in an instant, surrounded by swirling dust, which began to clear with the breeze.

'How is this possible?' he yelled, tugging. 'How is this hap—'

A gag appeared, snaking around Fredric's mouth, so tight it locked him in a painful-looking smile.

Without a word Tim sat down, cross-legged, on the warm ground beneath. A laptop materialised in front of him, arriving as his fingers lowered to type. Next to that was a small satellite connecting it to the internet. He plugged in the memory stick and, within a minute, the loading bar was full and footage of Fredric's confession had been posted online.

The truth was set free.

A few paces away, Samantha and Dee were bewildered, even scared, both clearly wondering how he was doing this, how he was creating things in the real world.

'Tim,' Samantha said, her voice quivering. 'What ... what's going on?'

'I can do it,' he said. 'I can make anything ... anywhere.'

'How?' Dee asked.

'The reader.' Samantha pointed to her own head. 'When you recalibrated it in the control room ...'

'Yeah ... I ... maybe somehow, the ... the technology fused, did something to me. I feel like I'm in the imagination space.'

'This is serious business,' Phil said. 'I submit a visit to a GP might be apt.'

'But … otherwise … you're still all right?' Dee asked, cautiously stepping closer.

'I think so,' Tim said, scanning across the flat desert, heat waves turning the air to jelly towards the horizon. 'I'm just … thinking outside the box.'

'I was honestly going to say that myself,' Phil said. 'But I thought better of it.'

Looking down at his hands, Tim could feel it. He knew. Whatever he imagined would appear. He had absolute control.

'Mind over matter,' the monkey added. '*That* is what you should have said.'

Chapter 19

On the first evening of the Easter holidays Tim, Dee and Phil ventured up to the edge of Pine Common, where the long striped fields sailed down the valley back towards Glassbridge. Up here they could see for miles, even further when they lay on their backs, on the ground, and looked up at the clouds above.

The past few weeks had seen the steady return of normality – or as close to it as they were able to get. After they'd stopped Fredric, the army, police and some men Tim assumed were FBI agents arrived at the facility. The remaining bear-sharks were tranquilised by some extremely confused animal control workers. Their weighty, sleeping bodies were loaded on to flat-bed trucks, covered with tarpaulin and driven God knows where.

The authorities, understandably bewildered, arrested them all. Fredric, Tim, Dee, Samantha and Phil were driven to a strange military base, deeper in the desert. They were kept in separate cells and faced seemingly relentless interviews by suited men with earpieces, poker faces and a distinct lack of humour.

Eventually, they were allowed to go home.

Professor Eisenstone's release from jail was a triumphant moment. Tim and Dee watched from the back of the car as he strode out of the prison gates a free man, carrying a small suitcase and a worn expression of sheer relief.

'I feel I might be doing something wrong,' the professor said, greeting them both. 'Indeed, ending up in a cell is becoming quite, quite the habit of mine.'

Tim and Dee explained what they'd done, the efforts they had gone through – firstly to get the box back and secondly to clear the professor's name.

Later, Tim told Eisenstone about his new 'ability'

– his apparent total control over physical matter. However, while he was able to prove it by creating a few objects on a small scale – a carrot, a marble and a fortune cookie – he struggled when he tried too hard. He supposed it was the stress of the situation that allowed him to restrain Fredric and that, without such raw necessity, he would need to practise.

Nevertheless, the professor was both astonished and alarmed by the news. He told Tim he would need to study him for answers.

There was still a slither of guilt when Tim thought about what had happened – of course, it all started with him taking the imagination box to school. However, when he apologised to Eisenstone, he could tell that all was forgiven.

'Tim,' the professor had said, 'every mistake is a single step down the wrong path. As a consequence, indeed, the right path only glows brighter.'

The familiarity of Elisa and Chris's attention had been comforting in ways Tim couldn't comprehend. After everything, it seemed strange to feel a sense of absolute security in the simple fact that they *were* interested in his well-being, now no longer under the command of that nefarious technology.

Following the confession, which was spread globally by Samantha's news report and prime-slot documentary, people took to the streets in crowds to celebrate smashing their IcoRama phones. Headlines, TV reports, radio, the internet – everywhere seemed abuzz with what had happened. As a result, shares in Wilde Tech plummeted and the company dissolved. Fredric himself was imprisoned – a photo of him, stubble-faced and shamed, became an iconic sight around the world.

Harriet Goffe's innocence was made public and she was reappointed as director of a reformed TRAD. Tim apologised and, to his surprise, there had been no hard feelings.

'Hey,' she said, 'these things happen.'

'Do they?' Tim asked.

'Well, no, but you know what I mean.'

The monkey's identity crisis was, as Tim had suggested, addressed to some degree by creativity. His pursuits led him to paint great, vast works of art which were framed and hung throughout the Dawn Star Hotel. Pride of place in the lobby went to his vibrant canvas featuring the pigosaurus rex engaged in mortal combat with a bear-shark (depicted in this case with, for some reason, wings) atop an erupting volcano. On Mars. It was really weird stuff and Tim was quite surprised Elisa allowed it to be displayed so prominently. To be fair, all his paintings were well-crafted pieces.

The monotony of school had reared its head again and, although what had happened with IcoRama was common knowledge, Samantha insisted that Tim and Dee stay anonymous when it came to the coverage.

'You don't want fame,' Samantha had said. 'Trust me.'

School had been alive with the news and many began showing off their replacement phones. However, Tim and Dee stayed quiet, closer now than they'd ever been, bonded by another shared secret that, to an outsider, was no more than a glance and a smile from across the classroom.

Without his imagination box, Tim was back to

doing his work the old-fashioned way. Although, of course, it often sucked, there was still a certain pleasure to be had from honestly attained achievements. After all, he knew better than anyone the plentiful pitfalls of getting what you think you want.

As for Samantha, her career was boosted dramatically by the biggest story of the year and, before long, she was a household name. She even had her own show.

On a cool, fresh spring evening, she invited Tim, Dee and Phil to visit Park Ridge Cemetery. Samantha had a small bouquet of yellow flowers and a special gift in her pocket. It was an unusual setting for a reunion, but somehow still jubilant. The cemetery was surrounded by bold fences and bare grey trees which reached over the boundaries like curious hands – Tim saw buds and the beginnings of leaves arriving amid the twigs. They strolled down the long, straight tarmac path to her husband's plot. Samantha placed the tulips on the grass in front of the granite stone that had, around its base, the early shadings of moss.

'Joseph Locke,' the engraving read. 'Loved and missed, taken too soon.'

'I told you I'd find the truth,' Samantha said, rolling her hair, now longer and back to a natural brown, behind her ear. 'Hiding in plain sight.'

She then removed a broken IcoRama phone from her coat and, after digging a shallow hole in the turf, slid it inside. Tim watched her pat down the mud, then return to her feet, before hugging him and Dee in turn. They left the grave, the yellow tulips still visible as they passed through the gate. Samantha didn't look back, however. Not once.

And so today, atop the hill, Glassbridge spread out before them, Tim, Dee and Phil were lying on the uncut grass admiring the clouds.

'That one's an old man,' Dee said, pointing. 'An old ninja man.'

'I am afraid I cannot decipher such an image.' Phil frowned.

'The top bit is his hat,' she added. 'The plane trail is his sword.'

'Do ninjas wear— Oh my, jolly biscuits, I see it now.'

'How about this one?' Tim said, concentrating on some low wisps of vapour and sharing his imagination with them. He had practised a lot over the last month or so. Slowly but surely a picture emerged.

'That is ... It's a monkey,' Phil yelled. 'And he has a typewriter.'

'I wonder if anyone else is noticing these,' Dee said.

'Good point.'

Eisenstone had told Tim to keep his powers – if you could call them that – quiet, which seemed a reasonably sensible idea. The images above, thankfully, cleared by themselves, spreading and unravelling in the wind.

Purple dusk drew the nearby woodland shadows over them, but no one wanted to go home yet. The topic of what happened at Fredric's facility arrived, as it had done time and time again over the past weeks.

'When I thought you had died, I didn't care about anything,' Dee said. 'Literally nothing mattered. Not even drowning. It was as though the floor, the earth itself, had just become irrelevant.'

Tim smiled as she picked a long piece of grass from

between them, twirling it in her fingers. For some reason he found himself noticing her eyelashes as she blinked.

'I'd wanted more,' she said. 'More things. More toys. More clothes. More gadgets. More. But when I was sure you were gone, I just thought about all the things that matter, and all the things that don't ... I know what you mean.' Dee shuffled closer and rested her head on his shoulder as they watched the night arrive. 'It's just stuff,' she said, flinging the grass away.

Tim squinted at the clouds – he'd had enough of them for tonight. So he gently swiped his hand and the blackening sky began to clear, the early stars like glitter, almost flashing above them. The ceiling was truly gone. Now, looking up through the fire-white dots above, Tim could only wonder how far his imagination might take him.

Epilogue

Harriet Goffe was fast asleep when her mobile lit up, buzzing across her bedside cabinet. *BRRRH – BRRRH. BRRRH – BRRRH.* She flinched awake, apologising to her husband who rolled his pillow over his head.

'Yeah, what is it?' she groaned, yawning, stepping into the hall.

'Harriet, Harriet it's … it's Rick …'

Resting the phone on her shoulder, she wrestled her dressing gown on, tugging it up her arms. 'Who?'

'Sorry, Rick, Rick Harris.' He sounded flustered. 'I'm one of the junior lab technicians. I worked on twenty-two at the Diamond.'

'Oh, all right. How...' Another yawn – she rubbed water from her eye. 'How can I help you, Rick?'

'I ... I was overseeing the ... the filing of all the evidence from Crowfield House. The teleporter, we moved it when TRAD was shut down, but I carried on working on it. It ... I was looking at the software it uses. Custom made. It's ... it's impressive. There was data on it. Lots and lots of data. The code, it was from chamber A, you understand, and it was going to chamber B. But there is a glitch. Or there was. In the system ... so it didn't work. It never worked.'

'Excuse me, Rick, what are you talking about? Can't this wait until the morning?'

'No, not really ... I ... I fixed it. I just fixed the glitch. It was a simple line of programming. But ... the moment I did, chamber B ... it ... it came alive. Lit up like Christmas. The teleporter works and something... something appeared inside.'

Harriet flicked on the lamp in her hall. '*Something?*'

'Well, no. Some ... someone.' Rick cleared his throat. 'A woman. She said ... She said her name is Clarice.'

Don't miss the next

Imagination Box

adventure.

Coming soon . . .